IMMINENCE

IMMINENCE

Mariana Dimópulos

Translated from the Spanish by
Alice Whitmore

**TRANSIT
BOOKS**

Published by Transit Books
2301 Telegraph Avenue, Oakland, California 94612
www.transitbooks.org

First published in Argentina under the title *Pendiente*
by Adriana Hidalgo editora 2014
© Mariana Dimópulos 2014

First published in English in Australia by Giramondo Publishing 2019
Translation © Alice Whitmore 2019

ISBN: 978-1-945492-55-6 (paperback) | 978-1-945492-56-3 (ebook)
LIBRARY OF CONGRESS CONTROL NUMBER: 2021941135

DESIGN & TYPESETTING
Justin Carder

DISTRIBUTED BY
Consortium Book Sales & Distribution
(800) 283-3572 | cbsd.com

Printed in the United States of America

9 8 7 6 5 4 3 2 1

For Cecilia and for Sandra,
for the wise mistakes.
And for Beatriz.

I would have spoiled the whole story, for if God had returned Isaac to me I would have been in an awkward position. What was the easiest for Abraham would have been difficult for me—once again to be happy in Isaac.
SØREN KIERKEGAARD

WE'RE ALONE TOGETHER, for the first time. I have to touch him now. I try stroking a foot, then a shoulder. But no current lifts in me, nothing pulls at my chest the way they said it would.

The baby has a foot that shines silver from the wool of his bootie. I try again, but I can't even get close. Removing the covers, removing any of his layers, is suddenly unthinkable. I laugh to myself. I tell myself it's impossible, and the thought is like a soothing caress; nothing is wrong, it will pass.

Ivan comes into the bedroom and places his hands gently on my hair. He takes the bundle the baby is wrapped in and nestles it between two pillows in the middle of the bed. Only the baby's slightly red and perfectly round face is visible now, as cryptic as the face of a clock. Ivan tells me dinner is ready and the baby is sleeping, and logic dictates that since the baby is sleeping we can leave him. Logic, in my mind, has always been a woman dressed in white—white now has the lustre of a silver foot.

We both sit down at the table, but Ivan immediately gets up and plunges the ladle into a pot on the stove. He doesn't want me to lift a finger, he repeats, I have to take it easy after my month in hospital. It's early to be eating, only six in the evening, and the autumn sun is pushing boldly through the kitchen window, which is open despite the cold. I tell myself: this should make me smile, the last rays of sunlight.

So I smile.

'Is that the baby?' Ivan asks.

I don't know. I didn't hear anything.

'I'll go and check,' he announces, and gets up from his seat again.

He doesn't return for a while. I wait for him, dipping my empty spoon in and out of the bowl of tomato soup sitting before me. Then he returns, and he is beautiful like giants are. I would never say you are beautiful like giants. But if he asked me to I would have to tell him because a year ago I swore an oath, not an oath of love or fidelity or surrender or any of those grandiose lovers' vows but an oath to always tell the truth.

He asks me if there are enough nappies for tonight and I answer him truthfully.

'We'll have to change him later.'

'Yes.'

'We'll have to bathe him later.'

'Yes.'

He refrains from asking me if I will do those things. This is good.

'Don't get up, it's alright,' Pedro insisted on that final night, as I got up to fetch water from the refrigerator. We had just started dipping our spoons in and out of our bowls of tomato soup. Then he stopped. He raised his pair of brown eyes and asked me if I could hear that.

'Hear what?'

He made a face, got up and left the kitchen. He returned a little while later carrying the cat, black and drooping. He had rescued it by the tail from atop a dangerously unstable washing machine we kept on the balcony.

The apartment is silent and the soup is still hot. Ivan starts speaking to me:

'I've been thinking. I wanted to tell you. The baby's name is Isaac.'

'Isaac? I don't know.'

He lifts his eyes—the same deliberate motion with which he'd lifted his body minutes earlier. His eyes are made of snow and water. They have their own sky and their own passing clouds.

'Isaac was my grandfather's name,' he says.

Coming from any other man, this would have struck me as vulgar. The unexpected revelation leaves the two of us momentarily perplexed. Isaac is a name without *r*'s; every time he says *Isaac* he will miss the dark, musical *r* of *roses* and *radios*.

'You don't like Isaac?'

'Isaac is fine,' I reply, and I touch Ivan's arm.

Was he the first? No, there was another. At a bus stop, waiting for the 132 early one morning, after leaving Pedro's place, I met a man whose name was also Isaac: dark and sleek-skinned and carrying a map under his arm like a baguette. We boarded the same bus just as the day was cracking open. Not long after I sat down, the seat to my left became vacant; with a smile that was like a gesture, the man sat down beside me and unfolded his map. The fact that the day was just beginning united us in a kind of fleeting complicity. I warned him against all the nonsense he would hear about Buenos Aires from the mouths of guides and well-meaning bystanders, as if he were the last witness left on earth. I took care not to embellish at all when I told him the name of a building, or the name of a street, and if behind it there loitered some national hero or calamity; then there were the theatres and banks and the interminable commerce of the city, interminably announced by all those interminable signs.

'Are you getting off here? What a coincidence,' he said when he saw me shouldering my handbag.

We walked a few metres together.

'That sweet shop is over a century old,' I pointed out, because I couldn't see anything older to offer him, and old things are always of interest to travellers.

He asked me for some figures I didn't know, and didn't dare to guess. How many people, how many deaths, how many trains. The man named Isaac had a familiar weakness for numbers; he had been named after Newton. He seized his opportunity and suggested we get something to drink in the shop. I said yes, because I'd just come from another man and needed curing.

'Ladies first,' he said as he opened one of the bevelled glass doors.

'I'm not a lady,' I explained.

'A woman, at least?'

'I'm not a woman, either.'

Pedro laughed, Pedro clapped his hands together in the middle of the street, Pedro tried to embrace me when he heard my confession. It was our fourteenth date, and at the end of it I told him the thing that had been weighing on my chest like an impotent talisman: 'This isn't meant for me, I'm not one of those women.' When he heard this he glowed with a radiance I'd never seen on him before. We were heading down Florida Street, fighting shoulder to shoulder for space on the footpath. We were coming or going from the cinema when he pulled me into a café and, against his better judgement, ordered (and was denied) a bottle of wine. Two cafés later we were finally seated. I drank the several glasses he handed to me. I did it for his sake, since I never drink. We got a little drunk on eggnog, drunk enough for him to speak loudly about our future, and his hopes for it; drunk enough for him to use the word *us*, insistently; so drunk, in fact, that when we left the café he left behind a handful of dusty, mildewed books, bought that same night from some dingy rat-hole on Avenida Rivadavia, now abandoned amid the several glasses we had emptied that evening.

He insisted on walking, so we walked. His happiness was incomprehensible to me; in his moments of silence I stole glances at it, and when he stopped and spoke to me I observed it directly, the way one observes a luxurious object—a feathered hat, for example, or an engraved ring— in a shop window. By the time we arrived at his place he seemed to have come to his senses. There was nobody home. With some pride he showed me the apartment's two empty bedrooms, as if to prove it. He lived with one of his sisters, who had promised to move out soon. He repeated this fact to me several times, perhaps because he didn't quite believe it; I tried to help him out by repeating it myself. When we took off our clothes and contemplated one another in the narrow bed, barely covered by the guileless, pitiless patterns of our underwear, he made me swear—although we both professed to be atheists—that I would stay there with him all night, that I wouldn't steal away in the early hours of the morning to catch the number 132 bus, or, claiming insomnia, sit at his desk doing sums, as I'd done several times before, perched carefully on the edge of the seat, at the edge of the desk, taking care not to touch a single one of the books or papers that cluttered it, humming out some binomial formula, some simple or complex derivative, like a lullaby. Pedro and I fell asleep, and suddenly it was all true: when we woke the next morning it was morning, the sun was up, and we drank imported teas for breakfast, and the teacups were the same teacups, and we didn't break any of them, and his sister still hadn't returned and I was still there.

Ivan asks now with his eyes, which are two polished stones, if I am enjoying the soup.

'*Soil?*' he says in Russian, and I say no, I don't want salt.

I suspect we are not like all those other lovers sharing dinner tables across the world, the many millions of them, the many more than millions that have existed throughout history. I am suddenly struck by this suspicion, which I don't deserve. I say *ah*, without making a sound, and watch as Ivan sprinkles *soil* on his tomato soup. We're not like anyone, I think to myself. And I am wrong.

'Water?' says Pedro.

The cat was sprawled like a dog beneath the dinner table.

Now I think: I shouldn't be thinking this, this is not good, this radical idea, but it's already there, I have just thought it, just a moment before I walked into this kitchen I decided that happiness exists, and as I practise this unfamiliar happiness, which I've been doing for the last couple of hours, I realise the extent to which this same happiness might anaesthetise me, blind me, chase me away, as it does everyone else, all the time.

The water from that other night is equal to this night's salt.

In the age of good sarcasm, in that first flush of youth, Mara used to say that the stork doesn't come from Paris.

'She comes from Baghdad, with a bullet hole in her breast, and her feathers are so black she looks like a crow.'

And Ludmila would applaud in delight.

I don't know if I can do it. In the month and a half we were in hospital I couldn't bring myself to do it once.

After the birth, after the infection and the convalescence, with my sister at my bedside and my mother in Las Flores, both of them crying as if this were our final farewell, after hearing my sister sob for the twentieth time 'you're so pale' or 'you're so thin', grasping my fingers and lifting my listless arm like a dead snake, after all of that I was finally able to sit up in bed, to slurp at the custard flans and purées offered to me by the unsmiling nurse. But at no point was I able to touch him.

This morning he arrived in his transparent baby carriage. One of the women lifted him up with a movement that was somehow both gentle and decisive and placed him between my lap and my chest, arranging my body just so on the cushions. But even that didn't work—they removed him straight away, muttering the only possible explanation: you're still too weak, what a shame.

'Nonsense!' Mara said to me a couple of years ago, stroking the hand I'd accidentally left lying on the table. Then she leaned forward, towards a little mirror with a stand that perched on top of her knees, and painted her lips and eyelids. Those were the early days, not long after our reunion, and it was fascinating to see the lips limned with red pigment, the mouth puckering and stretching, the upwards-rolling of the eyes. If I replied: 'I can't do it, I'm not one of those women,' she would plonk me down in a chair and stick her fingers into different creams and powders, employing soft little brushes where necessary, and she would draw all over my face while contorting her own into shapes of mockery or concentration.

If they were still doing dress rehearsals, she would come off the stage and sit with me. Her dressing room was just a plastic desk in the corner, a few steps from the wings, concealed behind a folding screen and illuminated by a cruel lamp half hanging, half falling against the glass of the mirror. She would say (and later she would repeat it, although she was no longer in the play):

'Father died exactly a year ago, on this very same day, on the fifth of May, on your name day, Irina. It was very cold, and snow was falling.'

This, and a few sentences more about a father we didn't share, and a Russian snowfall that neither she nor I had ever seen. When I refused to go along with it, she would say: 'You know this one, it's Chekhov, it's the three sisters.' Perhaps it was her way of talking about Ludmila, who we missed, without having to admit it. When Mara arrived at the theatre or if I saw her in the street beforehand she would never greet me with a hello, she would say: 'Father died,' or 'It was very cold, and snow was falling,' and I would have to reply:

'Why do you insist on remembering it!'

It was a half-hearted game—each player indulged herself as she saw fit. Then we would hug, because she was large and invited hugs. This was only after our reunion, mind you; we'd known each other since we were very young, but then we'd grown apart.

On the day of our reunion, Mara arrived and asked me if I could still love her. I told her I didn't know, because a lot of time had passed and I was used to telling the truth; or rather, telling the truth was the only thing I knew how to do when I opened my mouth and it wasn't to yawn or to eat. My 'I don't know' was enough for her. We went out together that night, and other subsequent nights. If it was a Wednesday we went to the city, if it was a Tuesday we met at the theatre, and if she insisted and it was a Saturday we would relocate to one of those places where men and women offer themselves to each other, brandishing wineglasses like expensive jewels. If she caught me in time she would force some brushstrokes against my eyes and lips, and if I protested with something like 'It's not necessary, I have something to tell you, I'm not a woman,' she would rebut with her usual 'Nonsense!' and grab me by the arm, and off we would go.

At the beginning of it all, at twenty and twenty-one—that is, twenty years ago—Mara and Ludmila and I would talk about coupledom, that thing fashioned from the bourgeoisie and love, as if it were polar ice, or the black floor of the ocean. It was a relief to think of it as something fantastic and unreachable.

'Is that the kid?' Ivan asks again. The dregs of the soup are a red tongue at the bottom of the bowl.

We haven't spoken about his last trip, the one he took to Catamarca or Jujuy, in a truck this time, punctually delivered by the mechanic on Avenida Warnes just a few days after I was admitted to hospital. I know it wasn't a trip he took for pleasure, it was something he did so we could afford to pay for the furniture in our apartment because tonight, if we eventually manage to get to sleep, it will be on someone else's mattress on the floor, our clothes still bunched into bags beside us—his because he just moved back in after all the comings and goings to Minsk and to the Argentinean provinces, mine because I only just returned from hospital, after the birth and the massive infection.

Ivan has decided it's not the kid; the sound is coming from the street. He asks how my sister is. She was here just earlier, she brought me home in the taxi and walked me to the front door. She handed him the baby so I could get up the granite stairs without tripping over. Since this isn't an important question, I respond with something simple. Ivan serves himself another bowl of tomato soup.

But no, he's not convinced. He gets up from the table. He gets lost in the hallway; in reality, he simply walks down the hallway; it's not even that the darkness swallows him up, or that he disappears into the darkness of the hallway as if into a gaping mouth. I know he's gone into the bedroom and that soon he will reappear through the same door. I decide it's best to stay where I am. The only other option is to follow him into the bedroom, where I would have to take the baby in my arms and say foolish things to it.

That other night—my last night with Pedro—suddenly returns, dancing like a blowfly.

Pedro, too, got lost in a hallway without getting lost. Then, like now, I remained sitting in the kitchen, like a teacup or a loaf of bread.

Ivan is away a long time, and I can't help speculating: he must be running a bath; he must have found a cockroach and he's trying to catch it. But no, I tell myself, it's autumn, there are no cockroaches.

I waste a good amount of time on this, thinking up explanations. It's not the first time I've been in a kitchen like this, waiting like this for a man, spinning those threadbare, faithful stories that women like me cling to in the hope of forestalling the abandonment that always seems to lurk on the other side of our waiting. I find comfort in it. I tell myself it's good to imagine bad things.

'He's resting,' Ivan says when he returns. His *r*'s are like ebony.

I get up and tidy the plates, but Ivan intercepts me on the way to the kitchen bench and gestures for me to sit down, so I sit down. Doing so gives me enormous pleasure. The hospital was exhausting, it's true. When Ivan turns on the tap to wash the dishes the water shoots out like lightning, then abates to a muddy thread that soon trickles to nothing.

Ivan announces that he is going to check the tank, and I follow him up to the roof terrace: there is a streetlight, bending between the buildings, that is yellow and functions as a late, miniature sun. We go up a little iron ladder and confirm that there is no water in the tank, that the tank is barren. Getting back down is a little more difficult. Ivan reprimands me for following him up there in the first place. Then we see the long arm of water tracing its way along the pavers below us, on its way to the drainpipe, which we hadn't noticed on the way up. Ivan knows what has happened even before he opens the door to the junk room. He says *junk* the same way he says *kid*—somebody must have taught him.

The blowfly of that other night needs shooing. Last time

we ended up with a dead cat, and nobody should die today. Or maybe the cat didn't die that night. Pedro was smart enough to take it away before I could find out.

At Celeste's place, too, the water always used to run out at the most inconvenient times. Downstairs, in Mr Sirio's real estate agency, we were constantly inundated with emergencies and calls for help, as were the plumbers and builders whose numbers were listed in a decades-old phone book Celeste kept bundled together with elastic bands. As we waited for the plumbers, Celeste would curse her sorry fate and the general untrustworthiness of tradesmen, upon whom she was forced to depend. She was exaggerating, of course, for my benefit; all her grievances were dedicated to me. She would bemoan the treachery of the plumbers until, finally, one would arrive, wearing overalls and a broad smile. Celeste would criticise the lead pipes that had never been replaced, and walk around the apartment as though it were a museum, muttering 'What about this rising damp?'; 'What about this crack?' and hitting the walls as she went. Before the plumber left he would always predict some further imminent catastrophe, accepting, as he did so, the glass of fizzy drink Celeste presented him with. If the two of us stood watching him sip at the glass, he would start to ask us questions: whether we lived alone here, in this big place; general queries about the building; if there wasn't too much of a draft at night in the windowless hallway. The plumbers weren't the only ones who craved the abbreviated version of a family Celeste and I represented.

With the water fixed we would dedicate ourselves to washing the backlog of pots and clothes, or boiling vegetables. It was good work and it was easy work. Back then I had a weakness for drawing polyhedrons and solving derivatives; nevertheless, in those first few days after the water returned, it was easy to peel and boil and contemplate the floating vegetables, with their foul cooking odours, and listen to Celeste dishing out advice for my future, that distant time in which I would *have a man*: Cut the pumpkin like this; Beware the secret poison of broccoli. And I was never lying when I said yes, and agreed with her; I wouldn't run and seek solace (as I so often did) in my numbers. I was never feigning affection when I kissed the soft peach fuzz of her sagging cheek, nor when I promised to cut the meat just so, the way she had showed me, or to cook the rice with the lid off, one day, when I *had a man*. They were all sincere promises, as simple as a shoe and its shoelace.

There is dark soil in the heart, fertile soil, where all kinds of thistles and flowers grow.

I tried it, with Pedro. After the formalities of sex we would lie stretched out on our respective sides of the narrow bed, in the thirty-five-square-metre, one-bedroom apartment we shared for a year. It was a precipitous slope that lead to the place we called *us*. From the top of the mountain the people below looked small and insignificant. We shared a bathroom, a dinner table, a bed. Pedro would use either the table or the bed as a desk, depending on his mood. Slowly he would unravel the long, rich fabric of his knowledge—of history, sociology, music—and big words would fall from his mouth like so many tiny crumbs. The entire world was a garden, through which one could simply stroll and ask oneself: 'What's this?' And the answer would be:

'Capitalism,' or 'Inequality,' or 'The consequences of the Treaty of X and the War of Y.'

At the end of that last night with Pedro, I put the cat in the box. I closed the box firmly and secured it with string. Then I picked up the knife.

Things are different with Ivan. Ivan is always right, but he is not like the others. He doesn't have opinions, or limitless knowledge; his wisdom doesn't belong to him, nor is it spectacular, like a Corinthian column or a syllogism. He says something and then it happens. 'The fever will go down,' he says, and the fever goes down.

We enter the junk room on the roof terrace, where Ivan keeps his mountains of boxes and suitcases, and yes, it is flooded. As we open the door we see the water hastily carrying away a few loose papers, some tapes that will no doubt get stuck in the drain. Ivan doesn't say: 'Those will get stuck in the drain.'

He picks up a soggy box with a fur hat peeking out the top. It smells like a basement in here, even though we're on the roof. A second later, the lamp flickers out; the cables are wet. We have to look for a lantern. Ivan goes. I lift up a bag filled with clippings; I shake it, and at the bottom I hear the clink of something metallic. I look through some of the boxes. When Ivan returns with the light, I inspect the bag again and see that the metallic things are rusted Soviet medals, although it seems the rust was not caused by this particular flood. Ivan takes out one of the newspaper clippings and confirms:

'These are from *Pravda*.'

I didn't know there were more of them. The only Russian newspaper clipping I knew about was the one he keeps tucked neatly between his documents and some bills in an old leather portfolio.

On the wall there is a large poster with drawings of everyday objects and their names, for Ivan to practise his Spanish. In the middle of the poster I see a large fish, with an eye like a tunnel. We rescue a few bits and pieces by placing them on top of a table, and our feet get wet. Ivan laughs, and I copy him.

'This.'

Ivan picks a medal up off the floor.

'Is true.'

'This is *real*,' I correct him, although I'm not in the habit of doing so. I have always thought (though it is a brief *always*, barely longer than a year) that in translating his words from Russian Ivan speaks better Spanish than anyone I know.

We have to go back downstairs as soon as we finish rescuing whatever we can; a few fur items need drying, as do some of the Cyrillic newspapers. So we rescue whatever we can, and we store them safely in a dry box. Ivan thinks we should also take the metal ladder downstairs; he lifts it up and carries it on his shoulder, as if it were tiny and made of plastic. He hugs and lifts the dry box. He makes me promise to come downstairs immediately, as soon as I'm done restacking the old manuals I'm holding. I promise, and I mean it. Then he asks me to add a few of the manuals to the dry box because he has a soft spot for the old photographs hidden inside them, the ones printed on tracing paper.

'What's this?'

'It's Chechen.'

A wet fur hat is about to topple off his treasure pile, and Ivan grabs it with his teeth.

My head follows him out the door.

'I'll be down soon,' I say.

In an old chest I discover some photos Ivan has never shown me. He once asked me not to look through his things, so I close the chest. He also asked me not to feel sad about his suitcases or his clothes, which surprised me, because until that moment it had never occurred to me that someone could feel sad about a suitcase. But now, inevitably, I do. One of the suitcases, I notice, is still sitting in the water; it has the air of a shipwrecked boat. I take down the poster with the Spanish words and the fish on it, and the fish looks at me when I point the lantern at it. There is no more water pooling on the floor. It's time to go back downstairs, like I said I would. To go and see the baby, to touch the baby. I should just start rolling, like a marble, and like a marble tumble all the way back down the stairs, unstoppably.

What an idea, the one about the blowfly. In that other apartment, Pedro's apartment, there was no roof terrace, no room of Russian things to cry over. They say everything changes, nothing stays the same.

An evening in Tigre: there we were, drowsing in a pair of deck chairs, watching the pier at our feet and the old tin streetlamp bending at its edge, with no globe inside its lantern and no cable to light it, thinking about the mosquitos and the climate the way one thinks about such things when one is outdoors and on a holiday, which is to say half-heartedly, or half-truthfully.

Pedro was reading, I was writing numbers on a grid in a book of puzzles. It was an evening like all the others we spent at the house in Tigre, which Pedro had finally decided to rent out of a professed love—incomprehensible in such a bookish man—of nature. Most philosophers went to the mountains and wandered around in the snow to ponder the death of God; not Pedro. Pedro preferred to ponder the death of God in that mundane, man-made place of pilgrimage, that barely exotic version of a jungle known as the Paraná Delta, a place he admired as if it were a painting or a prehistoric bone. We would stretch out in the shade and listen to the brown river, with the trees murmuring above us, and their murmurs seemed to me like the music of leaves. And we would be forced to surrender to the heat and content ourselves with the fresh, still air enveloping us.

On this particular evening, the punctual horde of mosquitos had already made its appearance. Pedro awaited them nightly, with the same anxiety he normally reserved for family visits. When they arrived he would serve himself a drink, or change seats restlessly. I would complain loudly, and smear myself with repellent.

We had been sleeping beside each other for a year. Only recently had we achieved the dream of renting the house in Tigre. That evening, I didn't bother to announce 'I'm going swimming', I simply got up and walked across the footbridge to the pier. It was going to be a cool night. Pedro had warned me that the tide was coming in, and as I approached the edge of the pier I could see that he was right: the last of the steps leading down to the water were already submerged in the river. I walked down and plunged in. I swam a few metres, then stood up among the reeds. A few boats passed by, loaded with women waving their arms around. The waning light winked affectionately, like a domesticated animal; it turned ochre and gold.

The light was iridescent in the evenings, Pedro said. I'm sure he must have written poems, and burnt them in secret at night. I know he called to me from the pier after I'd been gone half an hour. Then I saw him go back to the house, and later I saw the red glow of his cigarette in the garden, or the flame that lit it. When it grew a bit darker I got out of the water and climbed up the grassy incline behind me, which belonged to a house standing some distance away, behind a line of shrubs. Nor far from me, a boy and a woman were talking about the wickedness and the benevolence of bees. The boy was very confused by the fact that a bee had stung him. In the last light of the evening, they approached the place where I was standing. The boy yelled out first, as if he'd discovered an abandoned boat dragged in by the tide. He was disappointed to see that it was just a person; not even a monster. The woman greeted me. She said she recognised me from the evenings when we took the same ferry from the same side of the canal.

Was I swimming? She seemed curious.

We discussed swimming techniques, out of friendliness.

When was I going home? she wanted to know. It wouldn't take me long to cross the river again.

I didn't reply. Then they left, apologetically. I studied the river, thinking about width, depth, cubic metres per second, about how far the tide would rise in three hours, in six, in twelve, if there were nothing to stop it.

No turning back: a second-hand melancholy.

At Celeste's place, when she was still alive and then when she wasn't, it was so easy to turn back. To return. Sometimes Celeste would announce that there was a plant waiting for me: 'I've got a geranium,' she would say, as if geraniums were a big deal. And I would return, from school or work, to contemplate a plant I never watered. Other times she wouldn't say anything, and I would return to discover something new: two or three new heads turned towards me over the backs of Celeste's armchairs.

They would come from the provinces, from Las Flores or Junín; they were cousins or uncles, but usually they were quite young. Until she was well into her old age, walking stick and all, Celeste would go out of her way to look after them. She would suggest I show them the city, and some years I took three or four trips to the zoo, or to the theatre in Avenida Corrientes, to see some performance that invariably left them either in tears or stitches.

But that particular Cousin, the one who matters to this story, didn't sleep in the back room (the poorly ventilated one next to the kitchen). He didn't sleep in the blue room, either, which Celeste reserved for distinguished guests. We'd met many years before at a wedding. Celeste had put an awful black rinse in her hair for the occasion, which left two long, dark hoops of dye beneath her ears. The Cousin had sat at our table and played with the ashtray, spinning it around in his hand as he lobbed cheap pick-up lines at the woman sitting beside him. We didn't speak, let alone share a plate of dessert or comment like secret colluders on the quality of the steak. When the time came for us to leave he helped Celeste out of her seat, and as we got into the taxi he closed one of the car doors behind us and slipped inside through the other. Celeste doted on him all the way home, asking after his relatives in Las Flores, one by one—if she named one who had died she would sit in silence for a few blocks, then start up on a different topic: the family mill, or the Route 5 highway to La Pampa. At home, because of the wedding, both of the spare rooms were occupied. Celeste had chest pains and had to scrounge around for pills in a number of different boxes. The Cousin came and went from the kitchen, delivering water and coffee, as if he knew the place by heart. He had a long fringe that came down over one of his eyes, almost obscuring it, and with the two smallest fingers of his hand he made a little bow to fasten it, like an animal in the countryside.

Once she'd taken her pills, Celeste fell asleep on the couch. He wanted to know if I had sore feet, like most women after a wedding. I said no, but I let him touch them anyway. Then he placed his hand on one of my docile thighs, as though the hand were a discreet gift, like a ribbon, or a new perfume.

Mara and Ludmila didn't have parties. They didn't go to weddings or family gatherings, and they had sworn never to sign a piece of paper with any man. When they spoke about the future they would carefully weed out anything rose-coloured; they didn't believe in love, the way most young women do. In those early years of our friendship we used to meet up in a narrow one-room apartment in Once, near the Abasto market. The room was divided by a beaded curtain that every so often would emit a gentle *clinkclink* sound. Mara smoked rolled tobacco, forming cigarettes like miniature boa constrictors.

'To what extent?' Mara or Ludmila would ask. 'To what extent?' or 'In what sense?' or 'To what degree?' And, later, the other one (or maybe the same one) would add: 'It's impossible, there's no motive, it's pointless,' or she would say words like *interest*, or *selfish*, or *cowardice* or *boredom* or *fear*.

The night would fill up with words that they threw in the air like streamers. Their monologues were earnest, despite being peppered with the occasional joke. A man might call and nobody would answer the phone. And the man would leave a voicemail message that would have to be itemised and deciphered, like a message from a spy. They were masters of subtlety, and both possessed a scathing wit. And at the start of the night I would feel an enormous admiration for the two of them, and I would swear alongside them the sacred oaths of their master plan: I would never get married; I would never cry a single tear over a man who didn't deserve it; I would never have children, nor would I attend to any other such calls of nature, if indeed nature were ever to call.

And even though it was late, and the next day they both had to get up early and hand over several hours of their lives in exchange for money, one in an office and the other in a shoe shop, we would get in the car and drive across town to some distant neighbourhood, to Devoto or Avellaneda, and sit there in the dark peering through the windscreen to see if we could spot, in the illuminated room behind the window of a certain man's house, evidence of a woman who was neither Mara nor Ludmila; or on the rare occasions when we went out for a social dinner, the dipping of a pensive finger into a glass of wine; or, sleepless in a café late at night, the studious observation of couples assembled around a tiny table, a table like a lifebuoy, surrounded on all sides by the merciless ocean. At such times, Mara and Ludmila would analyse the situation from the corners of their eyes—her subtle gesture of boredom, his mumbled swear words—and they would conclude that she didn't love him enough, or he her, nobody ever loved anyone enough, and this was both good and bad. They would immerse themselves in mythologies, and buy books that, later on, they would dissect down to the very last letter, or never look at again. And I would smoke or read the newspaper or do sums in my puzzle magazines. And Mara, already a budding actress in those days, would go to the bathroom and come back, and bury her head in her shoulder, and announce that it was late, and because she was standing up, we would leave; because the bus was leaving, we would follow, clutching our purses close, and we would jump aboard breathlessly, laughing, because behind it all there seemed to be a strange kind of victory.

I'm still here, on the roof terrace. It's so good up here.

The roof terrace has new synthetic pavers, decorated here and there with little patches of tar. I cross it now as if it were an enormous desert, although it only takes three steps. A year ago, when I first came here, the terrace was paved with cracked red tiles, the kind I once saw in a dream—not a prophetic dream, nor a dream that revealed to me the secret of true love, but an everyday dream, because Buenos Aires is full of those red tiles. They were there on the patio at Celeste's place, and on the top floor of Pedro's building, where we went to hang the washed sheets. They might even have been at Mara's place, too. If a person dreams of roof terraces in Buenos Aires, you can guarantee she is dreaming of those same terracotta tiles. So it wasn't a prophecy at all.

I shouldn't come down from the roof. As long as I stay up here, nothing can repeat itself.

I come down from the roof.

I recognise the stairs as I descend them. The hallway
is filled with plants, and Ivan touches them from time to
time. I don't know the word for 'hallway' in Russian, or I
can't remember it, which is not the same thing. I linger in
the doorway of the bedroom: the baby is making noises like
a forest. I noticed this in the hospital too. 'It's because he
wasn't with you as soon as he was born,' my sister explained
earlier that evening. 'It's because you had that serious problem after the birth; if it weren't for that everything would
be perfect now.'

If the moon were out, and if the buildings were to open
a passage for it, its light would fall directly onto the pile of
nappies in this bedroom, each one decorated with cartoon
images of some wild animal domesticated by bright colours.
In the kitchen, too, a little earlier, when I got back from the
hospital, I saw on the bench and the shelves and next to the
sink other cartooned things, little cloths and bottles. The
baby moves his feet; neither of them are silver now.

Someone touches my shoulder: it's Ivan. Before I can
say a word, he says:

'The pants.'

The pants are part of the suit he came in. I didn't dress
him; my sister or some nurse must have done it. I ask Ivan
to do it, and he takes off the baby's pants. The legs are
exposed; for a moment I can't understand how they can be
so short and crooked.

'He's a baby,' Ivan explains. I must have stared for too
long. He strokes the baby's skin. Then, in triple time: the
seguidilla of the removed nappy, the salves and ointments
conscientiously applied between the legs, the new nappy
(which is torn), the fresh pants, because we decide the other
ones have been soiled. Now a cry rings out and fills our

lungs. I sit down in a barely illuminated corner of the room and shake my arms, which have started to tremble. Ivan brings him to me, saying:

'It's easy.'

That night when I went swimming in the Paraná river, turning back seemed difficult. The water had gone black. A long time had passed since I emerged from among the reeds and sat down on the grassy slope. Behind the shrubs stood the house that belonged to the woman and the boy, and when the breeze blew from that direction I could hear voices. I approached the house with the aim of telling who-ever was there that I planned to take the boat I'd seen on the other side of the hill, docked at a soft, almost decorative curve in the canal. It was hardly auspicious to emerge the way I did, from the shadows. I made my way towards a gazebo that had no doors to knock on; there were no dogs to announce my arrival, either.

The man standing at the barbecue grill pointed at me with the long metal prong he had been poking the meat with, a great sheet of meat that crackled in unison with the offal and the chorizos and a wholeaq white chicken along-side. The boy gestured at me with his arm, and the woman I'd spoken to earlier got up from her seat.

'Is it a ghost?' another boy asked, not much older than the first. I told them I wanted to take the boat.

'Ah, no,' replied a woman who was seated at the head of the table. There were wilted leaves on all the plates. A lemon, spinning like a planet, fell sideways. There seemed to be a whole collection of children and grandchildren present; a baby started hitting the table with a spoon, which prompted a high-pitched, passionate discussion on whether the baby should or should not be playing with a spoon, or with that specific spoon in that specific way, and whether his eyes, or his mouth, were or were not in danger. One determined woman seized the spoon from the baby's hand, and the baby complained and was consoled. Several minutes passed before the woman at the head of the table, whose long earlobes were clinched by two pearl earrings like a footnote, informed me that I was not allowed to take the boat unless I promised to return it that same night.

'I'll return it,' I said. I should have taken the promise a step further in order to gain her trust. I didn't.

'Who knows?' she said.

A fresh scandal erupted: a beetle had fallen into a bowl of something creamy, which one of the diners had been using to slather pieces of bread.

'Don't you have something to put on?' the woman complained, looking me up and down. The chorizos were ready to eat, it was the perfect moment to eat them; one minute longer and they would dry out, irreparably. They were promptly wrapped up in pieces of bread and passed around, leaving arabesques of oil on everyone's shirtfronts. The baby started to cry again, sparking a new discussion on possible motives. The only one who didn't participate was the woman I'd seen at the riverbank, an hour earlier.

The older children laughed at something and drank juice and Coca-Cola from glasses that were too big for their little hands, tracing ridiculous orange or yellow moustaches above their lips, where their future moustaches would one day sprout—although in reality they weren't moustaches, they were second smiles, reserved for the youngest among us, those who pay attention, who obey orders for years on end and omit what needs omitting and imitate what invites imitation, all in the name of survival, so they can eat and communicate, but never forgetting their subtle advantage, which is what inspires those double smiles in the first place.

The men concluded that the baby was crying because he was hungry; the women thought he was cold. Some time before, an unusually shaggy dog (unusual in this part of the world) had smuggled himself under the table. I'd seen it all from my place on the grass outside the gazebo.

The baby was wrapped up in a blanket and put back in his seat; various forms of mush were presented to him, on a series of plates. The proffered water was not to his liking, and was tipped over. The women spoke about child-rearing and childhood, they told tales of pregnancy and hardship in short sentences loaded with innuendo and exclamations. The baby was confronted with a piece of fruit, which he spat out. It was the heat's fault, it was the light in his eyes, the late hour, his age, his throat, his ears, this and that and the other. Ultimately, though, it was sex's fault, it was women's and men's fault.

'The dog has been licking his feet for a while now,' I informed them, because it was true. They had all forgotten about me, and I had sat myself down on a tree stump that had been converted into a table, but which I was using as a chair.

They shooed away the dog and the baby stopped crying; this gave me some leverage, but it didn't last long. The woman from the riverbank offered me a plate of food, which I turned down in case I had to swim back across the river. She had that beauty particular to women who have not yet discarded compassion and fear; she was nothing more nor less than herself, you could see it in her hands. Hers was not a beauty that could be idealised; it could never be painted or put into song.

'We'll lend you the boat,' she promised.

Pedro and I also toyed around with names, on our final night together, playing at Adam and Eve with the cat he'd brought home.

'Pupi, or Marx?'

At Celeste's place there was a cousin season, in the same way there is a rainy season. Celeste's home had been my home, too, ever since I came to the city from Las Flores. During the last stretch of my adolescence a bedroom door even bore my name—an austere insignia bereft of teenage embellishments. The cousins would come to stay whenever a child or a father was sent to Buenos Aires to be hospitalised, operated on, probed or studied in some big city hospital, which was invariably better than what they had in the provinces. Their sacrifice was a kind of consolation. 'We had to come,' they'd say with regret, and when yet another cousin arrived they would sit together in Celeste's living room and report, as if to a comrade-in-arms: 'I've been here for a month.' If it wasn't illness that brought them, it was marriage—usually someone from the more traditional branch of the family tree—or death. This time it was one of Celeste's brothers who had died. He was ten years her junior, which meant, even though he'd gone out in the simplest manner possible—grasping at his chest in the middle of the night—his death was classified as *tragic*, a word that was repeated several times at the wake.

There he was, standing in a corner of the room. This time he wasn't checking out all the women's legs, the way he'd done at the wedding. He was holding a white, unlit cigarette in his mouth, as if he were musing on something.

We hadn't seen each other since the wedding. A blonde woman was attached to his arm, it might have been her head or her hand resting on his shoulder, or perhaps all of her, clinging to his elbow as she stood beside him. We didn't even say hello. Celeste had cried her tears and decided it was time for us to leave. The next day was one of those hot, bright, breathless days, and we should have been following the coffin on foot through the Chacarita cemetery, Celeste shaded beneath an inappropriately pink hat with a big bow. But we stayed home instead, in front of the fan, until Celeste declared: 'That's enough,' and shut herself in her room to take a siesta. My schoolbooks were crowded with beauty: $x=2$, $a=3$. And yet, I couldn't shake the feeling that something remained unsolved, no matter how many pencilled calculations I made.

Later that afternoon some cousins arrived, spreading themselves throughout the kitchen, the living room and the bathroom, which was occupied for hours. They were the kind of cousins who removed cans from the pantry and butter from the fridge, without asking permission. Then Celeste, wrapped up in her dressing gown, insisted on preparing some 'real' food for them. He came in after the others had left, making no excuses for his tardiness, and accepted Celeste's offer of a coffee. He smoked at the window so Celeste and I could watch him. That same night, maybe that same moment, he invited me to go out for a drive. 'It's hot,' he offered, as an excuse. So we went out; the unsolved thing, the cataclysmic pull in my chest, which was little more than a response to my grieving thighs, to the agonies of the loins, demanded resolution.

In the car, the Cousin took my face and kissed it, which I appreciated. First he said what? then he said alright. After driving for about twenty blocks we stopped at a two-storey house with a sunken lounge and a non-existent kitchen, where a man in a bathing suit was fixing himself a drink. He immediately abandoned the drink in order to greet us with unwarranted ebullience, which for a moment I found flattering.

'We haven't met,' I said, but this didn't seem to matter to him. He must have been around forty-five, and I made an effort to avert my eyes from the ring of hair and flesh encircling his waist. The man didn't return to the drink he'd poured, which was left sitting on the coffee table; he later spilled it as he got up to fetch the glasses of Coke we hadn't asked him for. He was on a strict diet because of a trip he was taking, he explained; he had a few things to get through customs. He had a lively nose like a butterfly.

When the two of us were left alone, the Cousin told me about the rooms upstairs, which I agreed to take a look at. Before taking my clothes off I told him my full name, I told him I came from Las Flores, although he already knew that, and I talked about my mother and my sister, though not in much detail, omitting any florid or sentimental descriptions of the countryside or the draught horses, just enough for him to understand the face he was looking at; I also showed him the dog-like teeth crowded beneath my lips and the birthmark buried in my armpit. He didn't interrupt me once. He made a spectacle of his politeness; he didn't even touch his fringe, or make the little bow with his fingers. In my adolescence I'd acquired some small experience, mostly with boys my own age. But the Cousin was a man, and I had promised myself that afternoon, or at least that night, that I wanted to be a woman.

Drunk on forevers and nevers, Pedro would collapse into an armchair. He liked to have me close, at such times. Pedro was an intellectual athlete; thinking, for him, was like running. He would come into the bedroom all restless, coughing from so much thinking, and collapse into an armchair and close his eyes against a blanket. I'm sure he dreamed of strange kings and palaces; he was a man of monumental doubts, and no cathedrals.

After everything, and before Ivan: after Celeste, who was dead; after Ludmila, who was also dead; after Pedro, who had left, which is not the same but tastes similar: one day, framed in the doorway of my office, Mara appeared. She had duplicated her own face with makeup and fake eyelashes, removing the latter as she sat down. Every now and then she hugged a red bag to her chest, which was filled with outfits for a function. She had been gone for years, working in Caracas, she said; she'd forgotten about me for a time, and had enjoyed no longer having to think about me or Ludmila, who, as we knew, had had the gall to go and die on us. Then one day she asked herself: Why am I acting like such a coward? So she came home and opened or reopened the theatre, because—she now understood—deep down she had always been an actress. She shook her head as if she had a big curly mane, which she didn't. She asked if I could still love her, the way I did in those early days, when we were barely twenty, a decade or more ago. No, she hadn't counted the years; she wasn't like me, she hated numbers. Could I still love her?

'I don't know,' I replied.

'Have you had any children in the past ten years?'

But it was more than ten; at least fourteen years had

passed since we'd last seen each other. I gave her the answer she was expecting.

'I'm three months pregnant,' she said. 'I came to tell you, after ten years of not wanting to see you.'

'It's been fourteen years.'

I couldn't not correct her.

It was clear she'd established herself as an actress in the interim. She sat across from me, at my desk. I grabbed her hand, but it disobeyed me.

'You pity me. I can see it. I think it's better if I go,' she said.

But she stayed seated, and started saying all those things women say when they're glued in the yellow amber of their hormones. But the moment she verged into romanticism she fought it, quickly, like a fencer. She was suspicious, lurching back and forth between joy and some other state.

She said we should go, and we left, although the real estate agency was still open and I wasn't supposed to leave early. I lingered in the entrance because Mr Sirio was coming in, and I would have to give him an excuse. I told him the truth. He responded grudgingly. We walked out.

'I'd forgotten what you were like!' said Mara, throwing a heavy, happy arm around my shoulders, which she left there for some time.

Sitting opposite me, in the café-bar, she ate all manner of sweet and savoury dishes that were delivered to her one by one, on plates and in baskets. The table was good; not a dirty, black lifebuoy, swollen with seawater or tears, like the one those lovers (the ones we'd studied fourteen years ago) had sat around in silence, or in belittlement. There was no decay here, we didn't lie to each other the way those lovers did, our silence was not a form of blackmail, our future could not be held to ransom with some promise, and we each had a little paper napkin that we could fold however we liked, because, once our glasses were empty, we would get up and leave the folded napkins sitting right there on the table.

It was evening. Celeste sat with her chin jammed against her chest. She was sitting in her usual armchair, leaning forward. The smell of her cologne masked something else in the air, a whiff of something rancid beneath the odours of her body.

I dragged her to the dinner table. When she managed to balance upright in her chair, she asked me to paint her nails. We sat face to face, beneath the dining-room cobwebs.

There's a man, I told her, because I'd met Pedro.

There are a lot of men, Celeste said.

She'd asked me for the number 69, using her lottery numbers to communicate with me more easily. Her preferred vice wasn't a sexual position; it was tobacco. She sat smoking, inhaling deeply. When she spoke the smoke curled slowly out her nose and mouth, like from an old steam appliance.

We talked about the shade of pink in the nail polish.

I'm useless, I explained to her, although she'd already figured that out.

She gestured with the tremulous end of her cigarette towards a nail I'd forgotten to paint.

Children scare me, I said.

That's not true, she said.

I don't understand families, I persisted.

And this one, Celeste said, indicating another nail. I'd painted her entire finger pink. I fixed it up with a ball of cotton wool dipped in nail polish remover.

'When I die,' Celeste said for the millionth time, and I knew what was coming next: we were not to bury her; we were to send three letters to three different addresses; we were to leave the apartment to Mr Sirio so the cousins could still come and stay, the good ones and the bad ones, the way they always had.

'I don't want any worms.'

I promised her we wouldn't bury her. I got up from the table and arranged the little bottles of polish and remover behind the bathroom mirror.

Ah, I can breathe! Everything is so different, everything is better tonight. The baby is silent. The baby is not a cat. And the air doesn't taste bad, the way it did at Pedro's place that night.

Shortly before Celeste's death, Mr Sirio, the owner of several real estate agencies and properties, began making use of me, the way any self-respecting employer would. If he found himself in possession of a dilapidated old house he would convert it, if only for a few months, into a function room, or a ball pit for children's birthday parties, and I would have to dress accordingly, and act like a waiter or a babysitter amid the music and the roiling plastic balls.

One night Mr Sirio found himself in possession of a boat, which he rented out to a group for a social gathering. The boat had been tied up for years at a dock in Olivos, and its owner, who owed Mr Sirio money, had agreed to let him use it for the night.

People started filtering in; it looked to be a night of more or less phony euphoria, among friends or alleged friends. Pedro arrived with a tall woman. They sat at a table under one of the portholes, and the woman's cleavage was like a perfect simulacrum of eternity. In honour of that magnificent vision of beauty, it seemed Pedro had made one too many promises; later on, as I served him a drink, I could see his pulse racing.

Everyone was talking about music, as though they were all under some kind of spell. One large woman was wearing a green stole that draped down her back; one man was wearing an unnecessary hat. As I approached the table under the porthole, which stared out like a blind eye towards the black river, Mr Sirio stood up and grabbed me by the waist. He said he was proud of me, that he admired my love of numbers. He enjoyed engaging in boorish behaviour from time to time, but that night things hadn't worked out so well for him; none of his many lovers were on hand, and I was a decidedly bland substitute.

I went back to serving drinks in my mildly clumsy way. I served the man I would soon know as Pedro. Sitting there in his superfluous glasses, in the dazzling light of the cleavage with which he'd been entrusted, Pedro looked too stern—repentant, almost. He seemed calm and stable and alone.

The boat shifted, and the guests started jumping up and down to try and sink it. I retreated into the kitchen. Their laughter was only possible thanks to the proximity of the land and the concrete wharf to which we were all safely bound. As the night was coming to a close, Pedro intercepted me. He wanted a glass of something.

'I saw you at the real estate place.'

'Yes.'

'When I rented my apartment.'

It was an uncommonly dull conversation. The details of our shared past were minuscule, there wasn't much we could do with them. He tried again.

'So what's with the numbers thing?'

'Mathematics. And logic.'

'I don't know anything about that.'

He asked me for another drink. I spilled the wine half-way through pouring it. We both took the accident too seriously. We should have laughed it off. We didn't.

'There's a woman waiting for you over there,' I said when he asked me for a third drink. But he didn't go back to his seat under the porthole. Calm and stable though he seemed, he was running from something.

'You're confused. I'm not good at this. I don't wear dresses with plunging necklines. I don't even have a father. I'm not the kind of person who could buy a washing machine with someone, some day.'

Pedro left. Then, much later, as the wait staff were leaving the boat, I saw him. He was waiting for me outside, cleaning the lenses of his glasses, so he didn't see me when I walked past him. I stooped and said goodnight. It was a moment of weakness, and I congratulated myself for it.

An entire year had passed since our encounter on the boat, and Pedro was brushing my hair.

'Your hair's been a mess all night,' he said.

By this stage I'd learnt that such complaints were a kind of love, or whatever that thing was, like a vector or a wire, that bound us together, compelling us to call each other, to confess to each other, to care for each other, although not much of that went on at the beginning of our two years together. Lovers of books don't fall in love or write messages to their lovers all day: if a date had been made, it was met; if there was a party to attend, intelligent things were said or astute silences were observed. In that first year, before we began to share a bathroom and a bed every day, Pedro would invite me to his parties. I would arrive before everyone else and stake out a spot in a remote corner of the room, but it was never remote enough. Once the others arrived and assumed their positions I became painfully aware of the size of the living room, which couldn't have measured more than ten square metres in total, and how everyone was drinking from the same bottle, and my conspicuousness was unbearable.

Sometimes there were journalists at the parties, who laughed in the face of truth.

There were historians, both with and without beards.

The sociologists behaved like ladies at an old-fashioned banquet.

Later on some of them would get drunk, but only a little, because they were all over thirty and had nice three-bedroom apartments to get home to, fully furnished with a wife or a cat or both. Soon, Pedro would have those things too.

As he brushed my hair that night, Pedro was taking stock. He was somewhere between uneasy and satisfied. He had turned forty-one just a few days earlier, and perhaps he was secretly celebrating the fact that it was late and I was still up, sitting with him in the now-empty living room, listening to his plans: a house in Tigre, tenure, a few books he needed to buy, one or two he wanted to write, languages he wanted to learn. I nodded along, but not like one of those toy dogs that sit on top of the glove box of the car, with a spring in its neck.

We sat in the living room, then we sat in the bedroom; we went to sleep lying side by side, like adults.

I'd met his family that night. Pedro was happy, he had a woman. I had served everyone food, cutting generous portions, requesting opinions on the flavour of this or that, on the consistency. Just how Celeste, who was dead, had taught me. And those two people, scored with the wounds of some old injustice, those people who had engendered Pedro and spent years of their lives carrying and helping him, approving and disapproving of his appearance and his books, because he was bright, because he was young, because the world was his to inherit, said *delicious, delicate*, despite the radioactive hue of the apple cake, and they accepted everything I handed them, and they politely dried the corners of their mouths and announced when they were going to the bathroom. Pedro had foreseen all of this. He was relieved when they left, and as we sat in bed, finally alone, he looked down at the swirl of dark hairs just below his waistline, which seemed like a smile of satisfaction.

The best thing about a happy night is the way it bolsters us against bad things. If something bad happens on a happy night, we don't mind; we feel brave, there are cheeks and swords in abundance.

Due to too much jumping or running or singing onstage— or offstage—Mara lost her first pregnancy. It happened not long after she and her fake eyelashes appeared in my office at the real estate agency, seeking shelter in the doorframe. We'd celebrated our reunion, and her good news, by reciting the first act of a Russian play in an alcove of the café-bar.

Mara said: Father died exactly a year ago, Irina!

And I: Why do you insist on remembering it!

This scene was repeated several times over the following weeks, until one Tuesday when Mara didn't turn up at the theatre. The next day she announced that it was all over, and we went to a bar to take it out on a bottle of sweet white wine. Her grief lasted many months, during which time she emphatically renewed the sacred vows of our youth: she would never have children, men are worthless, society is a trap. Not even the simple freedoms, like sinking a hand into a lush green lawn or contemplating suicide, could console her. But the ideas she repeated were all marked, like cards in a bad deck. Ludmila's death was irrefutable, and fifteen long years had passed since our youth, which meant our convictions were harder to hold on to.

Every now and then Mara would turn up with a new theatre friend. Most of them were pale facsimiles of Ludmila. They would get fired up about washing the dishes, or the illustrations in kids' schoolbooks, or the way men drive cars and control all the money and care so much about machines. They would talk about the *penis*, the *member*, the *phallus*. They would say things like: Our greatest misfortune as women is that the penis is such a sincere, sensitive thing—it won't obey its owner, it only obeys desire. And they would say *penis* the way other people say *party* or *peninsula*: It's a *penis*! It's all the *penis*'s fault! If it weren't for the *penis*!

Some days the women were prisoners of their own inexorable natures, and they would declare this aloud as if they weren't—as if it were an objective statement. The thought of having to be attractive to a man in order to enjoy his company drove them mad, it was an unsolvable problem for our gender. It resulted in a lot of leg and a lot of bracelets. They all showed a lot of leg and wore lots of bracelets.

Ivan turns out the hallway light.

'So he can sleep.'

Above my head there is a number, an exponent, like a big bow, but I can't multiply it with anything.

We've been sitting in the dark for a while now. The baby is on my legs. Ivan tells me I mustn't fall asleep, that only the baby is allowed to sleep. Then he leaves, without touching the hallway plants as he often does. I sit there alone and repeat in my head the last Russian lesson I took before going to the hospital. I'm not surprised that I can still remember it; I feel proud.

The baby coughs and sneezes, but it doesn't cry. I listen to its noises and deduce that something is happening: the wheel in my chest starts turning faster, some rodent inside there is running like mad. That's good, I think to myself. I stay still, waiting for a feeling like compassion to rise up. It does. The baby's foot is not silver anymore, but in no way do I think of it as a foot that belongs to me, nor to anything that is mine. Still, I admire it, and I feel happy, as if its scandalous infancy were my own. But the foot is fragile, because it can't speak, because it has never even touched the ground.

I repeat my Russian lesson aloud: Fork, Knife, Spoon: *Bilko, Nosh, Lashka.*

I would like to be able to say to the baby: 'This foot of yours,' or 'This fragile little foot,' or 'This foot that has never touched the ground.' But I haven't learnt the word for foot, and I don't know any adjectives, and I'm not sure I know the verb *touch*, either. I try to get up and the baby wakes. I'll have to leave him in the cot. One of the nurses at the hospital told me he has to learn how to sleep on his own. Ivan isn't here to tell me if it's true or not true that the baby has to learn how to sleep on his own. I say: Come on, let's go, it's alright. But the baby won't stop crying, he's not paying any attention to me, and the words barely come out of my mouth correctly.

When we spoke, we got things wrong. It happened over and over during that year with Pedro. We tried, but we didn't know how to overcome our own eloquence. It didn't matter what we spoke about: hate, numbers, men; whenever we were together we inevitably wanted to *know* things, to be *right*. We would use big words that Pedro brought home from the university like souvenirs, or flowers, or pieces of furniture he found in the street on the way home. Then after a while he would fall silent and I would fall silent and the bedroom would become an immense pond. And the next day we would read a book or a headline that contradicted everything we'd said the night before. It's true: when we spoke we got things wrong, but if we stopped speaking we ran even graver risks.

My second night with the Cousin, after the time in the stranger's house, was in a pay-by-the-hour hotel. I was too dressed up for the occasion, and needlessly so; accessories are always unnecessary on a twenty-year-old. I had to keep pulling down my skirt when it rode up, like a woman at a wedding, and my blouse was equally troublesome: the neckline flapped open and shut like a book. On the ground floor of the hotel we were greeted by a man with a certain Wild West air about him, only without the cowboy hat and handlebar moustache. The man notified us of the rates and handed over a key. I wondered how many impatient couples started groping each other in the miniscule elevator.

'It's cheap,' the Cousin said, without touching me.

We spent a long half-hour considering one another in the

hotel room. There was a kind of chair to one side, made of green leather, but it wasn't really a chair. The entire ceiling was a mirror. I went to the bathroom wearing my shoes, and when I came out I wasn't wearing them anymore. From the bed, still dressed, the Cousin told me to take off my clothes. I asked him why, in complete earnestness. I told him I didn't understand why he wanted to see me naked. I said there's no mystery: this is tissue (I had already removed my blouse) and these are muscles (I poked a finger into the flesh of my leg). My bravery must have come from the authenticity of my youth; both Ludmila and Celeste were still alive back then. But then the moment passed, and I finished undressing, and naïvely fulfilled all the requests a thirty-year-old lover makes of a woman almost ten years his junior. And afterwards, the Cousin was so generous with me; he blew his fringe out of his eyes and told me about his travels to countries I'd never heard of. He meted out his cruelty in small, digestible doses. He was cruel to himself, too, and to humanity; lying there in the plastic-wrapped bed he told me about drug traffickers and elephants, mistrusting himself all the while, making me promise never to believe him. He was cynical and radiant, and I nodded peaceably, resting my chin against his ribcage and looking into his eyes.

Some of the women called it the *damsel*, at first; and later, the *wolf*. The more scientific among them stuck to the technical term: the *member*.

They would all drink beer long past dessert time, laughing or not laughing, but always exhibiting some brand of joy, a joy that wasn't reversible and didn't come wrapped in cellophane. That year, every dinner party began with the phrase: 'If it weren't for the damsel...'

Mara was the only sad one, in the beginning. I was working at the real estate agency.

'If the damsel doesn't feel like it, if the little wolf isn't hungry...' and so on, and Mara would elbow me gently in the ribs, who knows why. Later, Mara got sick of being sad, and grew tired of those women who barely dared to get drunk. She asked me to take her to the clinic, although I didn't have a car. She insisted it was a once off, but I went with her every time after that, too. I accompanied her through the second implantation, which failed early on, and through the third, which took. I was there for every check-up. We started going for walks together on Thursday nights, after the theatre. I started staying over at her place— this was about two years ago, now—and as she vomited I would eavesdrop on her excursions in and out of the bath-room, from behind the closed door of the guest bedroom, or from the living room, if the moon was out, because like her I had a weakness for that hypnotic, insomniac light sometimes described in fairy tales as *enchanted*, but which most people simply describe as *beautiful*. Mara would try to describe the strange things occurring in her body, although I never asked her to. She leaned like a tree towards certain increasingly sentimental theories on womanhood, and pos-sible baby names. If she said *Tadeo* I would nod in approval. I'd do the same if she said *Teodoro*. And when she was given time off after five months, due to her advanced age and the chequered history of her womb, I moved in with her. It was a great privilege to hand her a cup of herbal tea, or a piece of toast, and say 'It's getting cold,' even when it wasn't.

Extravagance: peeled potatoes, cooked meats. We believe, wrongly, that once we've discovered the big box of excess and smiles, of loving care and feminine devotion, we will never reach the bottom. And we believe the box will never close.

The milestones were met: Pedro and I shared a bed every night of the week, and I had already served his parents dessert. Suddenly, there were new dawns on the horizon. Tiny, useful things, like pencils and hairpins, had started to proliferate, infinitely. Each night I would perform the miracle of the loaves in the kitchen and Pedro would wash up and rinse out the dishcloths, talking all the while about those cathedrals of his, foam flying from his hands and mouth, and there was both panic and enthusiasm in his voice.

One year later we were in Tigre, and I was stranded across the river, waiting, and nobody would give me a boat.

Politeness: something I rarely practised before meeting Pedro. I'd tried it a little bit with Celeste, when she got sick, and occasionally on public transport, but that was easy—it just required standing up at the right times. Anyone with legs is capable of standing up politely. Being able to stand up is no challenge at all.

The night I went swimming in Tigre, Pedro and I had been together for two years. In that time I'd learnt a thing or two about politeness; if I hadn't, I would have simply turned around and left the family arguing in the gazebo, walked over to the boat, and taken it without permission, and nobody would have been able to stop me. But I didn't. I couldn't just dive into the water, either, and swim home. I did suggest this, once everyone had finally settled down at the table to eat. The last to sit was the pair of adults flapping like moths between the table and the grill, and the pair of teenagers relentlessly kicking a football to and fro on the lawn; finally they gave in, grudgingly flopping their bodies into seats, weary of having a family, baring their sweat-glossed chests and scratching themselves like apes. I took pleasure in a sudden pang of pity: one of the kids dressed in blue was crying over a piece of bread that had fallen on the ground.

'I'll just swim back,' I said from the grass. I bade them an almost feminine, almost sing-song farewell. The men got up and shouted no, they could not allow it.

'Most definitely not,' added the woman seated at the head of the table.

'Matías will take you in a bit, once we've finished eating.'

'It's really not far.'

'Is someone expecting you?'

The woman from the riverbank signalled to me. She freed up some space on a wooden bench, removing the drinks that had been sitting on it and drying it with a tea towel—unnecessarily, it turned out, since I would soon dampen it again with my wet bathing suit.

'You'll have to put something on,' the woman at the head of the table said, raising her fork.

The conversation turned to television and education; all or most of the diners apparently disagreed with the ways of the modern world, as if it were a foreign thing that didn't belong to them. The couple sitting next to me revealed another baby, a rather large one, seemingly out of thin air. They took turns holding it in their arms before depositing it clumsily into a gigantic pram filled with plastic mobiles and rattles. I was handed some cutlery, which I used very well. I nibbled like a bird at a piece of bread, and accepted a few vegetables and also some meat, but only a half serve, which is what women do. I didn't drink any wine, and I used my napkin in the appropriate way.

'I'm Sabrina,' said the woman from the riverbank, placing a hand on her chest.

She spent a long while sketching out the relationships between everyone at the table, which took shape before me like lines in an atlas. I didn't make a single calculation, nor did I start talking about paradoxes; I said no to sugar when I was given the chance, and because I was cold I accepted one man's offer to lend me a sweater, which he then proceeded to tie around my neck like a scarf. I blushed and didn't say a word when, after the wine was finished, some of the diners started blurting out phrases that were deemed inappropriate by some of the others. 'There are kids around,' someone protested, and for a while they resorted to double entendres in order to discuss the sordid details of some recent tabloid scandal, which I pretended to be familiar with. If anyone had asked, I would have told the truth: that in fact I had no idea what they were talking about; that I was unmoved by the little pastries an apron-clad woman had just deposited in the middle of the table, to resounding acclaim. But no one asked, so I leaned over to pick up another napkin, I praised the chef, I said yes and no when the conversation turned to diets, and yes and no when it turned to fashion, and a man was polite to me, and I apologised for asking him the whereabouts of the bathroom.

When I returned to the table I noticed that the spot next to my plate had been decorated with a glass of champagne, and I clinked glasses with everyone who offered. I made eye contact with everyone, as convention dictates (and as we were reminded by the woman at the head of the table); even with her I played the eye contact game, and also with the sweater man. The woman from the riverbank, Sabrina, coiled her necklace around one finger. One of the teenagers got up and left the table. After his departure, the teenager's parents spoke about him as if he were an indecipherable riddle they were greatly intrigued by, in spite of themselves. Some chocolate bonbons did the rounds. It was all so untidy and so possible, despite the poor deductions and logical fallacies. I promised myself then that I would go back across the river and say to Pedro: On the other side of the river there is a house, and I love its vulgarity; let's do it, let's invent something completely unoriginal, like men and women do.

Years later, on that fateful drive across the pampas with Ivan, in a town lost in the middle of the desert, another woman said another Matías would take me somewhere.

That means nothing; it's just a coincidence.

Renting the house in Tigre had been something of a second-last resort, though neither Pedro nor I knew it at the time. The cat was our last resort.

Pedro went away to his conferences, he gave his classes, he wrote for different journals, he read the same two or three books over and over again for months on end, Greek or German or Latin texts, parts of which he could recite by heart, like people did in the olden days. He kept at it, despite the constant disapproval of his colleagues, despite the eternal bibliographical grudges he bore. And all the while he thought about Tigre, that place to which he dreamt of escaping—both before and after the getting of the house— to *think*.

Kindness: some women say it grows on its own, like a weed, once you have a child. But sometimes a man is enough. Or a brother. Or a sick friend.

Pedro had theories the way other people have lice. He liked some more than others. He would pick at them, admire them, and discard them. Pedro's theories had been robbed of their ancestors; he disguised them, more or less expertly, and then repeated them like an old nursery rhyme. Sometimes he would say in a booming voice (pausing for drama, since he wasn't averse to theatricality): 'Man is the animal of animals.' Or, mid-shower, if he'd forgotten his towel again, he would yell out to me, and I would open the bathroom door to deliver the forgotten towel, which I would hang on the rack above the toilet. And Pedro, as if teasing himself, would say: 'One time is no time.'

And I'd walk away, because the steam was choking me.

'Are you there? I said that for something to truly happen it has to be repeated.'

'Aha.'

'But what about death?' he would say, poking his head out from behind the shower curtain, wet like a dog.

What about death? Or hunger? Or secrets? he would ask, if he was feeling especially jubilant, drunk on that particular tonic of his. He thought he'd accepted that the place he was in now was the place he was destined to end up in. On the horizon, like boats or clouds, all he envisioned were more journals, and the same old university.

In that year we spent living together, on certain afternoons when he would wake up from a siesta and insist on telling me about his dream, one he believed was full of valuable insights requiring our immediate and collaborative

interpretation, the alternating current between us was dis-
armed—that mysterious current whose units I could not
name, the one that made me admire and pity him in equal
measure, and misunderstand him, or fail to understand him
at all, and see him as utterly alien.

But I didn't always see things so objectively. With
Celeste, in death and also before; with Mara, both before
and after her pregnancy; with Pedro, on several occasions
and at different times of day, over the course of those two
years we were together, the first at a short distance, the
second under the same roof; with all of them it was enough
simply to look away, to think about the third binomial formula, or to say to myself $a + b$, $a - b$, and I could enclose
myself thus inside a magnificent parenthesis, where there
was no death, and no lost children, and no men.

I can hear Ivan now, in the hallway. I ask him to turn the
light on; I like looking at him. No, I assure him, the baby
won't wake up if we just turn on the bedside lamp, which
is on the opposite side of the large bedroom. He was
crying, yes, but then he went back to sleep. Ivan walks
over to the lamp, but he doesn't turn it on. Eventually
he leans over and picks up the baby and places him in the
cot and starts speaking to him in Russian; all true things,
no doubt. The old trinity of the nativity scene no longer
matters; I get up, although my legs are numb from sitting still for an hour, and place a hand on Ivan's shoulder.
Together we peer into the cot. This novel curiosity, which
I'm debuting like a new outfit, circles starrily above our
heads. Standing there in the dark we admire the kid (as
Ivan would say) as though he were a painting, and the kid
is good.

Ivan bends his head further and studies the kid from close up.

'He's vomited something.'

Ivan takes the kid back out of the cot. He's worried because I didn't notice the vomit earlier. He attributes the oversight to my lengthy stay in the hospital, and I trust him. We have to change his bib, at least. Ivan asks me to hold him, but I manage to run away to the kitchen in search of a new cloth to cover the little woollen pouch. Ivan puts the fresh bib around the baby's neck and places him for the millionth time back in the cot. I'm afraid he recognises my great weakness, so I start talking.

A year ago, in the desert, I say.

I start talking about the past, like a normal woman. I want us to exchange pointless sentences about the beginning of our relationship, because we're good together, because one day we won't be together anymore. My ears are itchy, and my wrists; I must be growing earrings and bracelets.

Mara was to blame. This was just one year ago. Mara put us in a car together, a car like a Leyden jar, and told us to cross the desert. Ivan's mission was to deliver the car north, to Neuquén; once we were in the city, I would branch off and continue on to Mendoza. That's how we met.

Mara knew it. It was the final season, the golden age of our friendship. We spent our time giving each other advice, like two squirrels on a tree branch. But it wouldn't last long. Mara was also on the last leg of her pregnancy; she had turned into an exquisite chest with only one piece of treasure inside.

She said I could stay at her cousin's aunt's place, in Mendoza. The aunt would make me go out for walks and pretend to be a farmer collecting fruit, but only if I wore a hat—I had to promise her I wouldn't step outside without a hat.

'What's so good about those trees?'

Ah! I never knew the trees in Mendoza were so special, Mara said. I would be a better person, she said, for touching a tree, for seeing a mountain; my hands would be better.

'It just hits you, like a ray of sunlight: happiness,' she said.

But it was all just an excuse to be alone with the baby. She didn't want any distractions when it arrived.

On the day Ivan and I were to begin our trip, we met up in a mechanic's garage in Avenida Warnes. In reality it was just the garage of an old house, plastered in car posters and motor oil. The meeting, which had been set up by Mara, was scheduled for the very early morning. I arrived on time; it looked like the mechanic hadn't slept either. While we waited for Ivan he told me some stories about numbers: the numbers grew fantastically and supposedly represented the earnings we could expect to make in a few months, if we continued in the car-selling business. I didn't bother explaining that I wasn't actually selling anything in Neuquén, that in fact I was going to Mendoza. I didn't want to dampen his enthusiasm. In a little pink book he'd noted down all the models that had been successfully delivered, and others he was thinking about sending out, and he licked his finger with delight every time he turned a page.

'So, is this guy coming or what?' the mechanic asked, once his numerical descant was over.

We sat down on a couple of wooden stools that chattered and squeaked, even when we were perfectly still. There was nothing left for us to talk about, so we listened to the stools instead. Ivan arrived half an hour later; he'd been waiting on the corner for quite some time, looking up at the street sign and checking it against the letters he'd written down on a slip of paper. The mechanic had seen him, too, but neither of us had said a word. When Ivan finally walked into the garage the mechanic shook his hand and laughed at him. He explained that the street sign was wrong, the numbering was actually the other way around. This error seemed to cause him insupportable joy. Ivan offered me a thick hand, which I shook, and said in Russian:

'Ivan.'

The mechanic walked us to the car. It was grey, slumped alone in a corner of the garage like a beached whale. There were a few technical explanations to go over, which we would in turn have to recite to the buyer. There were also a few tricks to learn, certain defects we had to hide once the car was delivered to its final destination. The mechanic stroked the roof of the car affectionately as he spoke. He handed us a bad drawing of where we had to go once we were on Route 22, which would take us all the way to Cutral Có.

As we got in the car, Ivan tried to fold himself up as much as possible. He looked enormous, hunching there behind the steering wheel.

'I'm Ivan,' he told me again, before we started off.

Getting out of Buenos Aires was entertaining enough. Ivan accepted my directions with a murmur of approval, which I'm sure must have meant something. He glanced over whenever I pointed out something curious on the side of the Panamericana Highway, something that would never have struck me as curious until then. Ivan seemed to transform everything we passed into a magical version of itself, like some kind of wizard.

'This is a factory,' I said, or 'This is a cemetery,' and I was overjoyed, as though death and machines no longer existed.

It's true: on that final night with Pedro I raised the knife and I stabbed it into the box.

'What are you doing?'

'It's so it can breathe.'

'Don't do that!' Pedro screamed.

The first time was with Celeste—the first time I discovered I could enclose myself inside that magnificent parenthesis.

For a long time, some mystery pain had been playing hide and seek inside Celeste's body. She spent her time calculating its whereabouts, adrift in a kind of daydream: now the liver, now the pancreas, etc. Her conversations with Mr Sirio, the owner of the real estate agency downstairs, and with the neighbour from upstairs (the one with the squeaky door), and even with me, had changed. She no longer mentioned, in that simple manner of hers, that she was eighty years old, as if this were some kind of error nobody had bothered to notice. She no longer said things like: 'I've got arthritis in this finger,' or 'I'm afraid it's my head, this morning.' That was before. Now, she just stroked her wide stomach after lunch, as if it held some kind of promise, but it was not a good promise.

'Hand me those pills,' she would say, and I always obeyed, although when I wasn't home she managed fine on her own. And if she insisted, I would clean (with toothpaste, the way she showed me) the silver cutlery that had been gifted to her as a young woman, and I would even scrub the kitchen windows, because it was the end, and she knew it, and so did I.

'Number 14!' she would yell the moment I opened the front door, and I would have to go straight back downstairs, armed with her neatly folded ten peso bill. Celeste needed no external or subconscious inspiration when choosing her lottery numbers. This was another of the liberties she took back then. She didn't have to see (or dream of) a drunk to know today's bet would be on number 14; she didn't need the flames on the stovetop to portend a number 76. Sometimes she would say to me 'Forty, forty-five,' and I would understand that she'd spotted the parish priest downstairs with his bottle of wine. Number 75 was a kiss.

Celeste didn't eat much, and every now and then she forgot forks existed. Ludmila had already been gone a few years, Mara had vanished to Caracas, and I had discovered that terrible, rancid sadness that almost seems uplifting but is only pretending to be; that resigned sadness that makes us conform to the way things are, and makes us say, with the worst kind of satisfaction, pushing our hair behind our ears, perhaps, or stroking the fabric of a jacket: 'Well, I guess that's just the way it is.'

No: the first time I put myself in a parenthesis, nestled safely between an x and a y, must have been with Ludmila.

Ludmila decided to die one night on a busy street that, as Mara would later put it, didn't deserve a face like hers, although that's exactly what it received: Ludmila's face, whole and perfect, crushed against the asphalt. I didn't shed any tears when it happened, nor did I seek refuge in abstract, metaphysical thoughts. I'd met the Cousin only a month earlier, at the wedding, although I'm sure we must have met at some point in our childhoods. Only a few days before Ludmila's death we'd sat together, the three of us, in Ludmila's apartment, a cramped shoebox in the centre of the city with terrible ventilation and a bulky armchair that interrupted everything. We'd absorbed several hours recounting more or less vain and inglorious anecdotes, his marginally more interesting than ours, for the simple reason that he'd lived a few years more than us, travelled to more places, suffered more cruelties. Ludmila was wearing a short dress, I was wearing a long one. She wore sandals, I wore sneakers. We'd been dividing our roles in this way for some time now, and we were happy with the way things were, and it was easy to be desired. We laughed at ourselves when we could. There's a whole world trapped, untouchable, inside those five seconds of a young woman's laughter. The open mouth is a grand landscape.

After several hours of anecdotes we finally ran out of things to say to each other, and ulterior motives were laid bare.

'I came to propose something to you, to both of you,' the Cousin said, very seriously.

'But you don't even know me,' Ludmila replied, standing up. It was the first time the two of them had met, and already they understood each other perfectly.

Ludmila made her way over to the other side of the couch, with some difficulty. He stretched out his hand to hand her the bottle opener that had been left on the floor, before she even had time to get up and rummage fruitlessly in a drawer in search of it, before she'd even taken a new bottle out of the fridge. She thanked him coolly, in typical Ludmila fashion. Fresh glasses of something were served and passed around.

'The thing you want…she isn't going to want it,' Ludmila said to him, pointing at me. She took it upon herself to distract us with stories about her boss's mistress, until well past three in the morning: she described for us in voluptuous detail the way the woman prepared for their clandestine meetings, how she dressed, the skimpy scraps of her underwear. The night had turned into a waiting game, and time had to be squandered if we were going to play it properly. The game was supposed to end with sex. I was the first to quit, noting that it was late and I wanted to go home. A proper excuse would have been better.

'Why?' the Cousin wanted to know. For a moment he seemed frustrated, then he half-closed his eyes, like a gentleman, which he wasn't, and stood up, because Ludmila was stuck again, between the couch and the bookshelf, right at the very top of her thighs, and with every contortion her body seemed to open like a flower.

'I told you she wouldn't want to,' Ludmila explained, beaming.

If he went downstairs with me, down the two flights of stairs that separated us from the street—even if he came running straight back after seeing me safely onto a bus—he ran the risk of being left with nothing. If his adventures in the Congo and the Marmara Sea had taught him anything, it was this one precious truth: once you've got a fish dancing at the bottom of your net, it's no good dipping it back in the sea to see if you can catch another. So he stayed upstairs with Ludmila.

In that year of mourning, the women sang: We must give; someone is in need, we must give.

That night in Tigre I returned from the other side of the river, after eating dinner in the gazebo, when a teenager named Matías (the first) got into the boat and rowed me across. It was impossible to know if Pedro had been waiting for me; his back was turned to the door. He was reading under his yellow lamp, the one he insisted on taking with him everywhere he went. He'd spent the first few weekends in the Tigre house rearranging the furniture, which was scant. The grass in the garden was wet from the rising river, so I made no noise as I approached; still, when I opened the screen door, which squeaked, Pedro didn't even turn his head. He was a great actor, talented at playing himself—in this, at least, he had always surpassed me.

'That was a long swim,' he said, but he was no good at irony, all his attempts came with a superscript that announced them. He invited me to come to bed. I apologised, to no reply, as we brushed our teeth, taking turns spitting into the plastic kitchen sink (the bathroom had little in the way of installations, just a toilet without a lid and a long shower neck protruding from the wall). I made a poor decision and offered him excuses, which is something I almost never do; I must have been running a fever that night.

I give up: I can't remember the first time I disappeared inside the parenthesis. I don't know if it was when Celeste died or a few years earlier, when Ludmila died, or if it was even earlier than that, in the countryside of my childhood, when some beloved pet dog got lost or poisoned, some dog I'd spent countless afternoons with, whispering childish secrets into his ears.

In order to pull off the trick, all I had to do was imagine a beautiful derivative. If that didn't work, I would make a little ball out of a stocking or a scarf and place it where I imagined the pit of my stomach to be, then spin around on the floor or the bed and wait for a few seconds, and soon enough it would start working, and any feeling even remotely like an emotion was swiftly eliminated. If tears threatened, the way storms threaten, if my stomach howled, or my throat, if the blood ran too quick and I needed to stop it, I could always turn to the scarf, or, in extreme cases, a fist pressed firmly against my diaphragm. The minutes of relief were precious; I felt like a tumbleweed, or as if I'd been hurled to the edge of the atmosphere. I became at those moments a celestial body, opaque and distant, untouchable, spinning weightlessly through space. But even before the hospital I'd promised never to use that trick again. Since meeting Ivan, I hadn't even thought about it once, it would never have occurred to me, not with the baby arriving in May. I had discarded the idea completely.

After the birth and the massive blood loss there was an operation, then several transfusions. A series of disasters. Then the septicaemia arrived to crown them all. I only heard about this afterwards. In the midst of my illness I would sometimes open one of my eyes, very rarely, like the lid of an old box: I would see my sister looking through the door of my hospital room, the same sister who never or almost never left the house in Las Flores, where we'd grown up, and I would be surprised, and I would think, *Something bad must have happened*, and then I would go straight back to sleep.

'Ivan will be back soon,' I heard her murmur to me, her face hovering above my nose. I thought: But where could she have met Ivan?

'The baby is alive' or 'The baby is eating,' she would announce. The updates trickled in over the course of several weeks—four, maybe five.

One day I said: 'Ivan?' I'd managed to sit up and drag over a magazine my sister had left for me on the bed, taking care not to pull at the drip inserted into the back of my hand. It was as if I had tentacles instead of arms. I recognised my own dressing gown lying on a seat next to the bed. I opened the magazine and read two perfectly empty lines of text next to a photo of a woman at a gala; I woke up and the first words I read were *in a striking green gown* and I thought aloud:

'Ivan?'

It sounded like someone was in the bathroom, or else the tap was running on its own.

'Is someone there?'

In other photos, people in phosphorescent suits were jumping around in the snow. Half an hour later my sister came in, with her simple face like a crayon drawing. She was pleased to see me awake; she came over and touched my forehead.

'Ivan?'

'He's away. He said he was going to Jujuy. He said he'd be back yesterday but we still haven't heard anything. He hasn't called.'

Who hadn't heard anything? Who was this *we*? Celeste had been dead for eight years, Ludmila fifteen. Pedro had left to be a professor in another country, forced to teach in a language he spoke badly, a language he caressed like a poorly trained and unloved dog. Mara had gone back into hiding, this time with her son in tow, and probably some new man or woman to share him with. My mother would never leave Las Flores. And the rest weren't worth thinking about.

I had to ask the question I'd been keeping under my tongue like a pill, like cyanide or ambrosia. All those nights in hospital had congealed into one night; I would wake up in the middle of that night as if in a forest, thinking the baby might be dead. I was scared, I was waiting and scared, terrified that he might not have survived the premature birth, or my long illness, although so many babies do survive such traumas. I'm scared for a baby, I'm scared for a man, I said to myself, and I felt pleased—after all those years, finally, I had done it.

Sacrifice: at the dinner table, it's so easy you can do it without even thinking. Ignoring a bottle if it's already half empty. Choosing the worst portion of food from a serving dish. Or the smallest. Or taking none at all.

I call to him now—*Ivan?*—in my woman's voice, barely demanding, which I've been perfecting since the day we met. Tonight, with the tomato soup, and the water on the roof terrace, and the rescuing of the medals and dictionaries, is the first of many good things to come, I promise myself. Everything will be new, like buds in a garden. I say *buds* and *garden* and there's nothing wrong with that, nothing naïve or pedestrian. But the baby doesn't want to get used to his cot, which is poorly assembled and wobbles a little. He starts crying again. I don't count the number of times he moves his right arm in the air, although in the past I would have done so with great satisfaction. I go out into the plant-filled hallway; only the stairwell light is on. The baby's cries grow softer and softer with each step. I go upstairs, I see that Ivan is back in the junk room on the terrace. I enter. I find him squatting before a box that must have remained on the floor, in the shadows, and is now wet from this evening's mundane little accident, which is such a good omen, because it will be good to complain together about the pipes, about the split tiles or the dead hot water system. Ivan has a medal in his hand.

'Another medal? I thought we got them all.'

'It's from the same time. My father's, or my mother's.'

I get closer, and peer over his head; he lifts a book and hands it to me.

'Dictionary.'

'Chechen, again,' I say, unnecessarily.

Now he stands up, suddenly, and asks 'What's that?' the way he did before, just three hours ago, when we were eating the soup of peace at the table.

'Is it Isaac?'

'Yes, he's crying, because he doesn't understand.'

'Doesn't understand what?'

Ivan looks at me with a scribble at the side of his mouth, a half smile about to fall into place. He could choose not to forgive me, but he forgives me right away.

'So, what are we doing up here?' he says.

Let's go, let's go. Don't I realise? It's Isaac!

Oncemore we are on the terrace. *Oncemore* we find a Chechen dictionary.

Late in her pregnancy, Mara revealed certain fears to me: that she wouldn't get along with her child; that they wouldn't love one another unconditionally, until the end of time. Perhaps Ludmila's old catchphrases came back to haunt her at night.

Mara was a woman who claimed to fear nothing; as soon as she felt a fear coming on she would turn her head, close her eyes, and in a single gesture she would become someone else. In that year of the lost first pregnancy and the second, successful one, I saw her turn into a peasant, or a surgeon, or an Aztec, with a flick of her wrist. All she had to do was start acting, and convince herself that none of the countless Maras inside her were afraid. Sometimes she would contort herself and say: 'I'm a duck.' I was always careful not to contradict her during these fantasies, nor to console her, as she would never have accepted either. All I had to do was gift her my laughter every so often, and she was happy.

When she thought about her unborn child, late in her pregnancy, Mara would occasionally perform lengthy exercises of fear, as if to prepare herself in case that other method failed: what if I don't understand the child, and he dies; what if I don't love him, and he murders me; what if he has a fever, or he's deformed, or he never laughs, or he has Benjamin Button disease, or he won't eat or shit or drink, or he comes out green, and so on. When her imagination got out of hand I would get up, go the kitchen, and bring her back some fruit, chopped in half on a plate. Then she knew it was time to stop. And we would play cards, instead.

Only later, at the last minute really, when camaraderie had made us softer and more vigilant—before her trial by blood (as she called it); before she sent me off in a car with a man, which was like sending me off in a spaceship—she stroked my hand, weary, perhaps, of the endless transformations, and resting momentarily in her true form—that of a woman, forty-two years of age and alone, or alone with a test tube baby, a lot of fruitless jobs, and very little money—she asked:

'What about you?'

'What *about* me?'

I understood her question, but as a rule we never deigned to discuss such topics; we never talked about the beauty of life, or the scandals of the next-door neighbours, or the shoes other people hid their feet in. We spent our time together in Ukraine, in Pomerania and Oslo—wherever the plays she brought home took us.

'That Pedro guy, he deserved it a little bit, right?'

I agreed that he did, a little bit.

'So why didn't you give it to him?'

'A child? Because there was no time. And anyway, I'm no good at that sort of thing.'

'We all think that.'

'Who does?'

I almost expected her to start eulogising the patterns on the curtains and pillows, and why not, since she seemed so intent on them; I probably would have followed her lead.

'Women!' she said.

'But I'm not a woman.'

'That's the stupidest thing I've ever heard. What are you then, a man? Are you a hermaphrodite, and you forgot to tell me?'

'No, it's not that.'

'Don't you dare grab that notebook.'

'Why not?'

'I forbid you to write a single number.'

And so on.

Celeste used to tell me: If you would just listen; If you would just set the table; If you would just use that hairbrush I bought you. While she buried herself alive in her litanies, I painted her nails at the big dining-room table in her apartment, which was also half mine. For some time now she'd been enveloped in a kind of dreamy revisionism, and she dedicated herself to talking the way she'd once dedicated herself to cooking and eating.

'I've been raising you for how many years? And now I'm about to die, and you'll stay here in that awful bare-bones room of yours…Not a single poster! Not even those horrible posters normal teenagers hang in their rooms! Nothing, not even a single photo, not even a photo of your sister, or your mother! And you won't look after the plants, either…After I'm dead they won't last more than a month, two at the most. They'll be lucky if they last two months.'

She liked to exaggerate. She did it to make me laugh.

Quite unexpectedly, Mr Sirio came into possession of a chocolate shop. I had to dress up in a red uniform, with a cap and apron. Behind me, sitting at the cash register in a cramped cubicle, was an overweight manager who spent the whole day whistling and puckering up his lips as he watched cramped merchandise. My job was to attend the narrow takeaway window that opened onto the street. The shop also had a large selection of jams and fruit-filled chocolates. Sometimes we ran out of one of the flavours. The problems in the chocolate shop were so simple I wanted to kiss them. 'We're out of cherry!' the manager would yell. And I had to find more cherry. We would call the distributors to no avail. So I would have to tell the clients, with deep regret, that at the present time cherry was unavailable, that I was extremely sorry for the inconvenience, and all the while the manager huffed on the edge of his seat. And that was that.

That night in Tigre, when I came home, Pedro and I had to talk, the way couples talk when they've been together for a long time, when they've known each other's physiognomy for years, and know how to forgive each other because

they've had to learn. It was past midnight. I'd already offered up all my excuses, which had fallen onto the table like
alms. So we pretended to enjoy a few glasses of the special
wine Pedro had brought expressly for that lover's week-
end—the first in which the house was actually liveable, in
which the roof no longer yielded to the rain. Pedro served
the wine from a bottle with a big label. He performed little
gestures and winks in the hope of enlivening what was really just a prelude to sex, which, like sleep, demands its
rituals.

'So you ended up having dinner with the rich neighbours.'

This was his way of demonstrating satisfaction, and
with that innocuous sentence we were on good terms
again. Half an hour had passed since my return from the
other side of the river, which I'd crossed on a boat with a
boy named Matías. I hadn't bothered to change my clothes,
and I still had dirt under my nails. Our wineglasses clinked,
the same noise my excuses had made as they fell onto the
table. During our year of cohabitation we'd taken a number
of precautions in order to avoid the uncontrolled skid into
domestic matrimony. We had no shared possessions—not
a single belonging that a registrar would bother to archive.
All we had in common were a few books; not even the
cups, not even the wineglasses we used that evening belonged to the two of us, since all of the kitchenware, as well
as the mattress we slept on, had been donated by family
members. We'd managed to avoid those peculiar, intimate
dinner parties at which couples profess before two witnesses
things they wouldn't dare say to each other when they're
alone. We didn't even use each other for company at the
cinema, nor for any of those other, all-too-common ruses
people come up with in order to cheat their way out of

loneliness and fright. Pedro would say 'Give me your arm,' and I would give it to him; Pedro would say 'I'll be back in a bit,' and he would remain seated, doubled over a book, with a hand against his forehead as if measuring a fever. And I would do exercises, or watch the television with the sound turned off. If he suffered, I would sit with him; if he sang, I would join in, although this happened only rarely. If he went away to a conference, I would wait for him the way I imagined any other woman would, monitoring the news and the telephone, half-fantasising in the night about terrible traffic accidents. But emotions dilute, like salts in a solution. If waiting was required, I waited; if desperation was required, I despaired. I was not expected to surrender to the evidence, only to love it, to say this hand, on the table, is evidence that we are together.

'I thought you'd just gone out for a quick swim. The Mulers aren't home, and I honestly didn't think you'd swim all the way across to the other side.'

The Mulers were neighbours of ours, from whom we sometimes bought tomatoes and lettuces after scrutinising the scent of each plant in their vegetable garden. They had a cat with yellow eyes and a stumpy tail, which would wade into the river with us when it was really hot.

The wine was good that night, and we laughed at my misadventure the way one laughs at the misadventures of childhood; it seemed so distant now, and we felt suddenly so brand new.

'You'll be thirty-six this year,' Pedro said as he served me another glass. What was the meaning of that pointless announcement?

The next day we went back to the city. We spent the remainder of the week promising each other that the following Friday we would head back to Tigre: we would leave the city after work, even if we had to drive out late, even if we had to catch the last ferry and walk in the dark and divine our way across the footbridges and alien parks, lulled along by the howling of dogs.

That's not what happened.

On the stairs, as we descend, the screams of the baby resound as if in a vault, and we quicken our pace.

The mother is to remain still most of the time, ever worried, poised to wake up if the child falls asleep, poised to stop mid-step, if she is running, ever ready to remove and to arrange and to groom and to wash.

'You'll see,' Ludmila would say, like the sybil she was. She would sit before us, nursing a cup of coffee, and predict our futures: 'You'll end up with a baby like a souvenir, at forty or forty-two—forty-three for you, Mara—because you'll feel the need to save yourself somehow, to disguise your own worthlessness; you'll have a baby because you don't want to die.'

Nothing could have survived long in such a harsh place.

Then she would call to the waiter, or look at herself in the little mirror she always carried in her purse.

Friday rolled around, and it got late so quickly. Both Pedro and I were relieved. The sky had played one of its tricks on us. We said 'storm', and sat back down.

Despite the laughter and the wine, our last night in Tigre had put us on edge. We'd been living under the same roof for a year, yet we hadn't cultivated any of those mundane conversations other couples seemed to master early on: conversations about whether or not the soap should go in the soap dish, if the wet towels smelled mouldy when they were left on the floor, if the bleakness of the refrigerator was the fault of neglect or insolence, and who was the guilty party. Our serene, lukewarm struggle against the spectre of separation, which hangs eternally over every shared thing, over every workplace and friendship, over the ecstasy of the sheets after sex and the red cards of our opinions, which we exchanged like playing cards, shuffling and re-dealing them every so often—all that had come to an abrupt end, or it was coming to an end at that precise moment, or something was impeding it, but it wasn't me, and it wasn't him.

The cat, which Pedro had brought home that week, was busy jumping from the table to the chair, getting some exercise. 'Someone gave it to me in the car park,' Pedro had explained. 'It's just for a few days.'

Now he was reading, with apparent difficulty, from a big green book—the Bible, maybe, or Goethe.

'Let's not go to Tigre tonight, it's late.'

'It's late, yes.'

'Let's make soup.'

Pedro sometimes suffered from stomach pains, although he would never admit it, preferring to perform a series of subtle manoeuvres in order to work his way around the problem. The green book, the red soup: both indicated that this evening he'd encountered some particularly hard-to-digest questions, ones that might even keep him up all night. What was the meaning of this, for example, or that? What were those pages saying exactly, *precisely*, at this precise point in time? Pedro's books were like countries, and they had to be traversed on foot. Sometimes he would get up and walk, scattering big words throughout the bedroom, the balcony, the hallway, letting them fall like storybook crumbs, although nobody would eat them afterwards.

'Kierkegaard,' he said. I had memorised some names by now, so I nodded.

The night began with a name, but it was retracted. Pedro changed tack:

'In Tigre, the other night. What were you doing? It was dangerous, what you did.'

'I felt like swimming.'

'With the river that high? I went out to look for you in the boat and I couldn't see you anywhere. I thought you'd drowned. Then I thought: She did it on purpose. Then I said: I suppose she's free to drown herself. Because you are, aren't you?'

'Yes.'

'You're about to turn thirty-six. And I'm forty-two.'

He didn't have any of the grey hairs one is expected to have at forty-two. He'd spent his life railing against neuroscience and bioethics and modernity in all its forms; he was robust, a man of convictions, a Marxist and a sociologist. He'd fought tooth and nail to defend what remained of his free will amid the asphalt of the capital; and now he was collapsing, like an axed tree, into the indignity of biological calculations. He'd finally accepted that, in the end, we are all just animals, and with his throbbing black animal nose he'd finally caught the scent of reproduction.

'It's three past ten,' he added, as if trying to placate me with this display of precision. Perhaps he'd decided to take one last detour.

But then the doorbell sounded, and I answered it. I was not expecting to see the person I saw on the other side.

'I'm going out for a minute,' I said, but Pedro had already receded behind the shield of his book. I took the stairs instead of the elevator. The Cousin was wearing the same shirt he'd worn to the funeral on Wednesday—one of our distant relatives had died, no more his uncle than mine. Along with the shirt, the Cousin came bearing an excuse in his hand, poorly wrapped in a plastic bag, and another one under his tongue, which unravelled the moment I touched him, spouting details about a tract of land our late uncle had left to all of us, and which I and the other cousins should agree to relinquish so that he, recently relieved of some or another business venture, could oversee and administer the property. I hadn't noticed it the previous Wednesday, at the funeral, but now I caught a glimpse of that loathsome, extravagant thing, somewhere between cynicism and enthusiasm, that crawled out of his mouth whenever he spoke. He suggested I sit down with him for a moment in the café-bar across the road, one of those big-windowed places furnished with empty pool tables. It would just be a few minutes, he promised. I agreed, and allowed him to buy me a coffee; soon we would be sweetly adrift. He opened the plastic bag just enough to reveal a glimpse of its contents, as if there were an exotic animal inside that might escape.

'It's a scientific calculator.'

'I can see that.'

'I brought it for you, I took it from our uncle's place.'

'You didn't take anything for yourself?'

'A few things, but nothing big, nothing as valuable as this.'

'Those things cost a hundred pesos at most,' I replied.

He looked surprised, said no way, I must be wrong. Then I smiled at him and thanked him for the calculator. Three of the buttons didn't work. So would I sign the papers? I agreed to sign the papers, which he extracted from a white envelope in his pocket. My share of the land couldn't have measured more than a quarter of a hectare, most likely all sand. I knew this, but he insisted on spending a few minutes searching for adjectives to describe how little the plot would be worth if it were separated from the rest of the land. He must have been giving all of us the same spiel, trudging from door to door each night in pursuit of signatures for the papers he kept tucked away inside that little white envelope. Would I ever go back to Las Flores? Of course not, he said, answering his own question. You'd be lucky to grow weeds on that quarter of a hectare. The minutes were jumping across the face of the clock hanging on the wall in front of me, surrounded by bottles.

'I have to go,' I said.

'No kiss? I won't let you go without a kiss.'

Duplication: when you have a child, the child will depend on you for its survival, the child will be unable to speak a single word. You will speak for the child, you will know, or believe you know, all its needs and fears. You will feel cold for yourself and cold for the child, or warm for yourself and cold for the child, or vice versa. You will have two hearts and two stomachs, at least for a time, and then forever, in a kind of beautiful, painful illusion. Try it. It requires effort, but it's not difficult at all.

I continued working at the real estate agency, after Celeste had died and Pedro had left. I would attend to the clients, over the phone or face to face, and to the tenants, who would come in to pay their rent with a wad of bills rolled up in a fist. 'But when are they coming to fix my hot water system?' they would say, or 'I've had no electricity for a week because the electrician hasn't turned up,' or some other testimony of urban misery, stuck in their one-bedroom apartments with no heaters and wonky doors. I would never respond the way I'd been taught to; I would say, for example: 'The electricity won't be back for at least two more weeks,' or 'That hot water system is ancient, nobody is going to fix that hot water system,' or some other such fact I knew to be true. Sometimes Mr Sirio would hear me and intervene, embellishing my opinions with some promise like the far end of a rainbow. He had tried telling me a thousand times, but I was unable or unwilling to understand: 'Look at their faces, for God's sake; there's no point telling them the truth.'

On the Wednesday of the wake of an uncle that I barely knew, from whom I would soon inherit a scientific calculator, I didn't spot the Cousin right away. A little boy had approached me in the entrance hall, claiming he wanted to ask me something. In fact he wanted to whisper in my ear the great secret of his name and age. He must have been the child of some relative who'd already gone into the other room to weep and pray. The child had been kicking a football right there in the hall. The people dressed in black and not-black continued arriving and vaguely greeting one another, ignoring him. Later, the child started playing all sorts of dirty tricks to try and win my affection. Since the setting was opportune, and since he was set on talking to me at any cost, the conversation veered towards life and death, and I won my small victory: I said all the comforting words we're meant to say to children about the future, erasing its finiteness with a single stroke, the way all adults do, with a single smile, with a gentle pat on the head; it was that simple.

I was left feeling elated. This was a new achievement. It was Wednesday. The Cousin had promised me, with a single sentence: 'I'm going to come and see you, I have to bring you some paperwork.' His face roused nothing at all in me. I was with Pedro, and I had just painted a five-year-old child's future exactly the way I was supposed to. On Thursday I felt just as triumphant, and I spoke to my new feline housemate the way crazy people speak to their own finger.

On Friday morning, when Pedro told me he'd found an owner for the cat and that I was to be liberated from my responsibilities towards it, I flatly refused, hugging the creature to my chest and shaking my head. I begged Pedro to let me keep it. At midday I went out; I spent far too long choosing a colour for the litter tray I planned to put in the bathroom, and as long again selecting an appropriate food bowl. I returned to the apartment Pedro and I had shared for an entire, somewhat radiant, somewhat unpleasant year; I still mistrusted the harmony of songbirds, but I was credulous nonetheless, treading lightly, telling myself, *why not?* And in the afternoon I brushed the cat and removed the thousands of tiny thistles trapped in its fur, then I patted it several times, making promises. This explains why I was so happy when Pedro announced we would not be going to Tigre that night, because it was too late, because there was a storm coming. He must have noticed the white hem of my mouth, the private glee of my teeth, as I concurred. In a single instant I'd become a giant, felling the trivial obstacles in my path, and the world seemed small enough to fit on a pinhead. Finally, I had it all: I could serve dishes and top up glasses, I knew how to get my hopes up, how to brush a cat, and tied to my wrist, like a red balloon, I had a precious reserve of compassion, always attached to me so I wouldn't lose it, so it wouldn't lose me.

Pedro was reading so beautifully, he was sitting so beautifully that last night, in the kitchen. I placed a hand on his shoulder and I felt an electric shock in my elbow. I confused the electric shock for everlasting love. Emerging on the horizon I could see a house, the ugly paintings we would choose together, then hang unskilfully against the wall. For a moment it all seemed so right. Then he started talking about Tigre, and our respective ages. Then the doorbell rang, and I went downstairs, and the Cousin was there with his black shirt, and then the coffee, and the windows, and the kiss, etc.

The baby is still screaming; its screams are a question, the longest question I've ever heard. Our job is to emend, to console, to convince.

When I came back up from the bar, after seeing the Cousin, Pedro was no longer seated at the table with the green book. The cat was nowhere to be seen, either. I looked for them, longer than necessary in those thirty-five square metres of apartment. At the end of the day, we'd made certain promises to each other. I found them both in a corner of the balcony. Pedro was balanced on the edge of a large flowerpot that housed an unworthy, emaciated plant; the cat was watching him from the branch of a nearby tree, wearing an expression of amused indifference, perhaps because it was just a kitten, or because it hadn't noticed the tortuous descent separating it from the pavement, ten metres below. It took all our wiles to coax the cat back onto the balcony, and when the operation was finally complete we laughed. The metallic pin that holds us together, squeezing our lungs and trachea and throat when we fear for something that is ours, had balled up into a knot, which the laughter released. This seemed like a good thing.

'What were you doing downstairs?' Pedro asked as we were sitting down to eat the soup he had prepared and served to me. The soup was tomato.

'Don't get up, it's alright,' he insisted when I went to fetch water from the fridge.

We'd only just begun dipping our spoons and in and out of the soup, when he stopped.

He raised his eyes and asked me if I could hear that. Hear what? He made a face, left the kitchen, and returned a little while later carrying the cat, black and drooping, which he'd rescued by the tail from atop a dangerously un-stable washing machine we kept on the balcony. This time we didn't laugh; it was as if the laughter vault had suddenly been drained.

'Who was at the door when you went downstairs? I saw you from the balcony, you were coming from the bar.'

'One of my cousins.'

'*The* cousin?'

A few months ago we'd fallen, feebly, into the trap of recounting stories of past lovers. The error occurred as a result of that false trust that arises, gradually, from the daily repetition of dinners and breakfasts, from the daily magic of saying *bread* and receiving bread, and the same thing with salt or wine or olive oil. All of this was glaring evidence of our life together, and neither of us would have chosen to deny it. The evidence was edible.

'Yes, *the* cousin. He came to bring me a calculator that belonged to the man who died the other day.'

'Your uncle from the country?'

'An uncle, yes.'

The cat was sprawled like a dog beneath the table. Then it got up and started rubbing itself against us, and Pedro scared it away with threats and clapping. When the soup was finished we went out onto the balcony to breathe the night air, and we regretted not taking the train to Tigre where, instead of traffic, we would have been listening wide-mouthed to the sounds of lapping water. It was then that we noticed the wind, and the bad smell it carried.

It must be a fire, we said; it must be a chemical spill. Hypotheses formed like dewdrops. We had spent other nights like this, and all the goodness of our words, all the friendliness of our legs on couches, had confused us, it seemed. It must be a boat over at the port, we said. But no; it was the end.

Isaac's cries ring out in long peals. Ivan looks up at me from the foot of the stairs; he reaches out an arm that has a red hand on the end of it, which I take hold of. We go down. We go into the bedroom. Nothing is wrong. We just have to do this and that, and this and that involve cloths and creams and jars that have been organised neatly on top of the cupboard by Ivan. The crying stops. Since the baby is now naked, Ivan examines him, out of pure clinical habit. He studies the automatic contraction of the limbs, which coil against the body like springs. Ivan offers the baby a finger and the baby closes his fist around it, like a carnivorous flower. The baby smiles, and I copy him. This surprises me, although really it's the most common thing in the world, and the world is so common.

'What's wrong?' I ask, for no reason.

'Nothing's wrong.'

And this is true, but it is a fragile truth.

Mara's women, with their tall bitter beers, during that year dedicated first to mourning and then to Mara's renewed attempts at procreation, would spend the evenings formulating hasty theories on what they saw as the fundamental aspects of life; they did so passionately, tumultuously, with that particular zeal of theirs, a zeal inspired not by fanaticism but by frenzied confession. They debated things heroically, trying to understand, without centuries of literature and philosophy to orient them, what it might mean not to be a man. They were eager, emboldened by the percussive bracelets flicking against their wrists.

After men, their favourite topic was children. Only a few among them had chosen to have children, and these outliers took great care not to betray a shred of maternal sentimentality in front of the others, nor to succumb to tactless arguments about *human nature*, and they never, ever, played the famous card called 'the greatest joy in the world', nor any card of that suit. One of these few, a woman with chaotic teeth and hair, had two children with a man she had loved but who was now dead, and she recognised, lifting her glass, but not to toast, that she'd felt nothing at all with the first child, but then with the second, when she held it in her arms after the birth, she felt a great sense of calm and relief, as if *she* were the one resting, cradled in her own arms, as if she'd just returned from some years-long pilgrimage on foot.

'How ridiculous,' they all said.

'What pilgrimage?'

Others, once night had fallen and the beers had been diligently guzzled, would sob that it was so good to get out of the house, it did them so much good; they were strong, but they weren't trees, they knew how to break. Mara would say to me:

'They're all so naïve. They think they're so...Who do they think they are?'

She preferred to talk about Oslo or Pomerania, about snow. She concealed her age and her desire to be a mother as if they were a heat rash, or an old spider bite, with creams and silk fans. Walking back to her place afterwards, she would continue:

'What *is* that, that aversion to being alone? That impulse to care for things, to nurse things!'

The act would take a while to wear off. There was nothing for it but to let it be; it was the inverse of her sadness, left over from that first lost pregnancy.

I look at the clock, which is smiling. It tells me the time is nine forty-five. I tell myself it's late, even though it's early. This, then, must be the thing I'd been both expecting and fearing at the same time, because why not? Worse things have happened, things more vexing to my Aristotelian logic. This new feeling, both feared and expected, travels from my legs to my pelvis and then up to my neck, working its way not up the spine but along the front of the body; it comes from inside and works its way to the surface, or vice versa; perhaps it is a bit like a wind blowing through me. Finally, it's happening. After the month and a half in hospital, in which I barely saw him; after those last two days of feeling well, awake in my hospital bed, talking, watching my sister as she brought me news, brought the baby to my door and showed him to me; then this morning, at home, and my sister handing him to me, holding him with me, and feeling nothing well up or release inside my chest, none of those feelings that are supposed to make us more than just flesh and bone. Now, though, it is finally happening. I pick him up and it happens. He has lustrous black hair, which I stroke, and it is soft, and his delicate head is mysteriously heavy. He closes his eyes and I close my eyes. He makes a face and I make a face.

I put the baby back in the cot. I walk to the kitchen in the dark, carrying a dirty cup I just picked up in the bedroom. I took it so I'd have something to give to Ivan, something more than my messy footsteps and head. My footsteps are so messy. I walk in. Ivan has his back to me. He is rinsing a cloth in the sink. An arrhythmic orchestra, electric and throbbing, rattles inside me. I sit down, ecstatic.

'This cup is dirty, too,' I say, as a way of saying: *I am here.*

Ivan takes the cup. He washes it. He puts more water in a saucepan. We still have to clear the table. I try to help him with the salt shaker, but I knock it over; I step on the dishcloth and rip it.

'What's wrong? Sit down,' Ivan says, stretching out his vowels.

'Where?'

'Your face is all blotchy,' he says, coming over to examine me.

'It's from happiness,' I reply, touching my left cheekbone, my nose, which don't seem to be in the right place.

On that final night with Pedro there was no roof terrace, but there was a balcony. And instead of a flood there was an acrid smell coming from the port or the city, which we inhaled and exhaled; it was one thing on the in-breath and another on the out.

Among Mara's women, there were two who were constantly chewing the ends of biros or their own nails, or the tips of coffee spoons. And when some older woman would sit down with us for the first time, ignorant of the rules of decorum, or intelligence, or independence, or impudence, and ask us one by one, noting our varied degrees of youthfulness with an expression of interest and commiseration, at once wanting and not wanting to hear the answer, in a pointless search for common ground, 'And what about you, do you have any children?' the nail-biter and the biro-biter would always answer: No.

'Ah!' the newcomer would say, and nothing more.

But the interrogated women would hasten to elaborate, clambering over each other to proffer explanations:

'We don't have time, and also we don't know if we really want to have kids.'

One was tall and was trying to be a ballerina, the other was an accountant and terribly enjoyed making decisions. If the opportunity arose for us to take a walk outside on our own, Mara would express pity for them, but only to a degree.

'They *think*...' she would begin in a sarcastic tone, but as we walked she would forget her gripes with the other women and become lost in her own reflections on how impossible it was, in general, to live in the world.

Months later, when she was about to give birth, she stopped talking about those other women altogether. Spring and summer had happened upon us suddenly, and we spent our nights alone, playing cards if we got bored. Mara had finally succumbed to the long-resisted daydream: she no longer worked or rehearsed, living off scraps inside the walls of a great palace, as though surrounded by lions and tapestries, and the child she carried was her only bounty.

One midday in December, Mara fell into a different trap. It took her forty years to say it:

'You know, you don't have much time left either.'

And the next day:

'Why did you let the oil burn?'

'You were talking to me, I got distracted.'

'You could have started a fire,' she said, stroking her belly the way she did in those days.

A spiral of flame had risen from the oil, and the apartment we almost shared was filled with the sweet smell of charred chicken, which was a nostalgic smell for anyone who'd grown up in the country, where we always burnt the chicken skins before eating them. Mara embraced herself in the armchair.

Her complaints were not completely hollow: I had recently let a couple of houseplants die, ones she couldn't water herself because they were too high to reach, and I'd let a few items of clothing fly off the roof terrace. It was also true that I'd started coming home later and later, cooking less, showing less enthusiasm for the shared projects we resorted to in order to pass the hours.

'You're starting to despise me.'

'That's not true.'

'You've gone back to your sums—I see your little pieces of paper, I find pieces of paper and I think: it's happening, just like before, it's all over.'

But no. All that really mattered was the baby's imminent arrival, and Mara was already planning a way to keep it all to herself.

If cousins with children came to stay at Celeste's place, I would try my best to teach them the times tables, or addition (with the help of a handful of oranges) or subtraction (with a handful of peanuts), and the cousins' children would roll their eyes, and someone would say 'It's too early, they're not even two years old,' and if it wasn't too early it was too late, because they were about to head out to see a movie, or to watch the clowns.

Just before the birth, and because it was summer, Mara said to me:

'You should go. There's a house in Mendoza, it belongs to an aunt of mine. I stay with her all the time. There's a lake. I can't go, but you should.'

'What about your baby?'

'It'll be red and wrinkly and it'll keep you up all night. You're a light sleeper, you'll hate it. Or am I wrong?'

'I don't know.'

I would have liked to tell her that she was profoundly wrong, but the truth got in the way. Long before I promised it to Ivan, long before I tried to hide it from Mr Sirio in the real estate agency and omit it from the occasional confessions I offered, like precious gifts, to Pedro, the truth had always stood before me like an obstacle. Ever since childhood, if such a thing exists or is worth remembering, I had experienced the opposite problem to most people: I found it hard *not* to tell the truth. The truth was like a cheap, colourful marble that I simply handed over. Numbers helped; everything was easier under the shade of a five or a minus four.

'The trip, the food, all that costs money,' I said, because I didn't want to go. I wasn't used to holidays, or spending money, and I hadn't indulged in either for several years.

'I've figured out how you'll get there: you'll go with a Russian guy. He's a doctor, or he was in the war, or maybe both. You'll drive there together in a car that has to be sold in Neuquén.'

She made a sweeping gesture, as if selling a car were like selling the whole universe, as if we were on the cusp of launching some huge enterprise, some honest, worthy, million-dollar empire, a thing we both knew did not exist. A friend of hers, an actor and mechanic, had saved himself from ruin by selling used cars in Chaco and Misiones, and he needed drivers to take them across the Puna and through the Andes; he wanted to expand his market, and it was a pity I'd never learnt to drive, and a shame (but not in the other sense of the word) that she was currently in the state she was in.

She made the universal gesture again, in reference to the thing hidden beneath her generous belly. There was no getting around it; in those past few weeks she'd transformed into one of those solemn, gravid shaman figures women inevitably transform into when they are on the brink of giving birth. She had to be obeyed.

That year of the beer-drinking women, I learned that several of them had given up men at thirty, or thirty-five, or somewhere around that age. They were already past the halfway point of their lives, heavily reliant on creams and powders, disguising themselves in all sorts of misleading clothing. Occasionally they would meet a man who seemed nice, or unscrupulous, and over the course of several dinners they would let their mouths and imaginations run freely as they discussed the man in question, in that predatory, wolf-like manner women adopt when they want a child, clearly and belatedly, the way one might want a sofa or a parrot.

I've just made some precious calculations: when he eats, change him; first bathe him, then dry him, then dress him, then put him to sleep, then wake him up.

A week after receiving Mara's orders, I found myself packing a bag for the trip to Neuquén. It was the same bag I'd used as a girl on my trips to Las Flores, and it had always been somewhat deformed. Many centuries had passed since I last went to Las Flores, so I had to dig for it at the back of the wardrobe. All I put inside were three articles of clothing and a pair of shoes. Then I made my way to Avenida Warnes and met the mechanic, and the car, and Ivan, who arrived late and confused, glued to his little slip of paper with the address written on it.

Early in the drive, I surrendered myself to new things. I, who never lingered on explanations, started giving them away freely, elaborating on whatever the landscape offered as we made our way out of Buenos Aires: the factories, the low-rise houses, the empty lots. I'd never been intrigued by faces, but Ivan's was different—it excited a festive curiosity in my chest, and I didn't know what to do with it. I couldn't wed Ivan's name (or face) to any number, nor could I reduce them to any formula.

'You're a doctor,' I said, and he nodded.

'You're Russian,' and he nodded again.

I didn't know anything more about him, and I didn't know how to make him tell me. I wasn't used to this:

I'd never had to ask these kinds of questions of Celeste, because I knew her by heart, or of Ludmila, or Mara, or Pedro, or the Cousin. And the rest of the world, after nearly forty years of being in it, scarcely mattered to me at all.

I'd confirmed something during my time at the real estate agency and the chocolate shop: people are constantly speaking to themselves, like so many talking dolls. Not Ivan. We drove along, me in my unusually open and determined state, he discreet and fantastic, like the unnamed creatures they say dwell deep in the rainforests and oceans.

'You went to war,' I tried. This, too, he acknowledged to be true, and I had to make do with his simple *yes* in response. Perhaps it was the language barrier.

'I don't speak Russian,' I said, although this was already painfully obvious, and pointless utterances had never been my forte.

Ivan turned his head to me and smiled.

In half an hour, my little world was turned upside down. I offered him a number of postcards that I thought were somewhat valuable, or at the very least not overly embarrassing: one from my childhood, adorned with a country house and a picturesque mill, and several others from later in life, knowing that he would never understand every word I used, for example if I said a word like *saccharine* or *subsidiary,* and maybe even simpler words, maybe even a word like *mill.* I told him about Pedro, although I shouldn't have, and about Ludmila, and her unequivocal beauty and how she'd died when we were twenty-two, and about Celeste's death, and about Mara, and how she used to imagine herself in Oslo, telling me all of a sudden: I'm rich, look at all these old faces.

When we turned onto the desert road in La Pampa I explained, with untimely enthusiasm: 'It's totally straight for the next two hundred kilometres, a lot of drivers get bored and crash.' It was noon, and the middle of summer, but the desert still displayed some signs of life—mostly sparse, low-lying shrubs. We could not, under any circumstances, allow ourselves to fall asleep, and the monotony of the road was our greatest enemy. There was nothing else for it; we had to talk. A few kilometres later, once I'd given up all my cards, Ivan started to offer me his. He said he'd been in two wars in Chechnya and knew all or nearly all the different musics of death: mortar, machine gun, pistol and fire and bomb and grenade. He said the desert was so beautiful, so much better than all that. These were clumsy comments. It wasn't necessary for him to make them, but he did, and I, sitting next to him, still as a statue in my seat, was grateful for them, inside and out. I thanked him several times. He might have read aloud to me from the list of Spanish words folded up in his shirt pocket, or counted to ten million, and it would have been worth listening to.

No, we couldn't turn on the air conditioning, or the radio; the mechanic had told us so that morning, because the battery was weak, the electrics were dodgy.

No, the rear windows didn't open, so we had to make do with the torrid stream of air that blasted across our faces, and there were no window shades to protect our arms from the blazing sun.

The water? It had spilled in the back seat, there were only two mouthfuls left.

These were all welcome hardships; the hot air brought with it a magnificent objectivity. Any other man or woman, had they found themselves on the same seat, beneath that same midday sun with that same blast of air, seeing and hearing what I was seeing and hearing, would have fallen in love with Ivan. What was magnificent was that I didn't have to do a single thing, just exist. I didn't even need feet, or a head.

'What's that?' I asked, because the song of the motor had grown familiar over the course of those seven hours of driving. Now, something was howling and whistling, and a light had ignited on the dashboard. We had to pull over.

The hands of the kitchen clock say it's three past ten.

'It's three past ten,' Ivan says.

After our breakdown in the desert, after all the confusion that ensued and then our eventual return to Buenos Aires, Ivan announced that he had the money, that he could finally pay for the flight, that he should have been in Minsk months ago. He still had a few 'things' to resolve across the Atlantic, on the other side of Europe. When he told me this his voice wasn't flaccid with the melancholy of the cold or the steppes or the cities of housing projects, although that's precisely what awaited him over there. I could already sense the journey in his eyes, the way one senses those journeys that aren't as simple as jumping on a train or a bus to the mountains or the beach for fifteen days of bad mattresses and food odours. Two days later we met up in a bar, on a corner next to a travel agency in Caballito, to celebrate and say goodbye, because we had only three days left together, and once we subtracted the hours spent working and commuting and navigating the general antagonism of the city, three days was a skeleton we could barely hang off. We ordered innocuous drinks and looked at each other across the table. It was the same table Ludmila and I had likened, twenty years earlier, to a lifebuoy— but no, Ludmila alone had said it, Mara and I had simply escorted her smilingly in her cynicism, and now she was dead, and she'd been dead for almost twenty years. This wasn't even a table, really, it was more like a four-legged impediment. I was triumphant: I made promises, I sent signals, I invested all my energy into calculating what Ivan was really trying to tell me, rummaging for the hidden meaning beneath every sentence, in a feverish kind of hermeneutics, trying to enthral him, letting myself become enthralled.

That pause, was it good or bad? His leaving a finger of coffee undrunk at the bottom of his cup must mean something. Everything was intertwined, as if in long wreaths. With my heart in this state, light and elastic, I looked through Ivan's bag when he went to the bathroom. I wanted to know what the tickets said about his return date, but the date was listed as *open*. When he came back I tried artlessly to figure out his intentions, but it seemed he had no definite plans beyond the flight itself: *Go, resolve, return*, three miserable, unmodified verbs, which he didn't even bother to conjugate.

No more questions, he said. Such questions are terrifying to men, when they come from a woman, and that's exactly what I had become: a woman. For two months now I'd felt this strange kicking in my chest. I was full of doubts about the future, as if the future were an actual thing that existed, and I had already observed with alarm the volatility that suddenly erupts in a man when he is desired by a woman, and he is only barely within her grasp.

Mr Sirio was a traditional Argentinean gentlemen, with his black cigarettes and his legions of buxom women, all coiffed and maquillaged to various degrees, who would appear with some regularity at the real estate agency and contort themselves before him in the hope of wrangling a decent dinner date, a night out that didn't begin and end in a single hotel room. At sixty-seven years of age Mr Sirio was proud of the circumference of his belly, encircled by a large belt from which, like all self-satisfied gentlemen, he dangled his pair of thick thumbs.

'Where's your make-up?' he would say to me. 'Where's your skirt?'

He found it vexing to have to retain me as an employee when I refused to cooperate; finally he confined me to the most remote office in the building, hiring replacements for the front desk in the form of a smartly dressed and perfectly effeminate young man and a young woman who didn't mind wearing proper heels.

'Won't you at least brush your hair?'

He'd gifted me a hairbrush at the end of the previous year. He always seemed more confused than offended by my appearance. But then he would throw a number at me, some tortuous number that he didn't understand, and I would return it to him clean and resolved, and he would have no choice but to forgive me for all the other stuff.

He's coming over now. He examines the blotches on my face, like a doctor; like a lover, he kisses them.

The doorbell rings, impossible at this hour, I think. But it's only four past ten. I stretch out my soft happy arm and answer it.

'Who was it?' Ivan asks. But he has his back to me. I pick up a plastic bottle with children's drawings on it, one of the ones Ivan prepared especially for our arrival.

The back of Ivan's head can speak and see, it is not indifferent like the backs of other heads. This has always made me happy—again, that brief, year-old *always*—but now it doesn't, because I'm about to lie to him and I don't want him to see my face when I do.

'Nobody.'

It's an awful response, which won't suffice if I want to leave the house.

'My sister,' I improvise. 'She came to drop something off before going back to Las Flores. Something I left at the hospital.'

I pause.

'It's an envelope,' I continue, almost enjoying it. 'An envelope and a bag and some flowers.'

I don't know how to lie, which explains how I set these ridiculous traps for myself. Where am I supposed to get those props? It's my first time lying, and I'm flustered; I put on a coat, I almost forget my shoes. A bat is flapping inside my chest, or a black banner. I walk down the stairs. I unbolt the door with difficulty, I'm barely familiar with the keys and they play tricks on me the way unfamiliar keys always do. Ivan leans over the banister and murmurs something to me.

'Got it,' I say, hurriedly.

I don't want him to come downstairs. The Cousin is waiting for me, one foot on the curb, one foot on the bitumen, and I approach him slowly. What is that smile he's trying to give me, like a feeble gift?

'Your sister gave me your address, I just called her. What a voice, she should be on the radio.'

He cast a few more spells of a similar calibre.

'I'm sorry I couldn't visit you in the hospital. I'm leaving town tomorrow, but I wanted to see you,' he says.

Just when I think it's over, he dares to ask the question.

'Where's the baby?'

'Upstairs, in his cot.'

'Can I see him?'

I should say something appalling, something magnificent, something grim, like *he's got six arms*, *he's blue*, since apparently I'm in a dishonest mood.

'No.'

'Does he look Russian?'

'No.'

'Can we go across the road?'

'What's across the road?'

'A café, can't you see it?'

'That's impossible.'

'The evidence suggests the contrary, my dear.'

He's right. Across the road there's a café-bar I've never noticed, despite coming here regularly for a whole year while Ivan was working on the apartment, refurbishing the kitchen and the roof terrace. The café has big windows and a long wooden bar lined with tea-filled whisky bottles. It reminds me of another café, but that's impossible. We go inside.

At a table down the back a dozen people are celebrating some kind of anniversary, overjoyed because someone or something has once again survived another year.

The Cousin uses all his wiles to convince me to take a sip from his glass, or at least to order a coffee. It doesn't work, but he isn't frustrated. The fringe of twenty years ago has disappeared, but the moustache he had last time I saw him, in Las Flores, remains, a black worm above his lip.

'You haven't responded to any of my messages this past month.'

The statement seems to amuse him, because he is a friend of adversity. I still haven't quite figured him out, and I get him wrong again.

'I have to go,' I say, simply, and get up from my seat.

Mara would have criticised my meagre efforts at defiance: the tone of my voice, my half-hearted gesture of resistance when he stands up beside me and grabs my wrist.

'I brought you something.'

He takes a white envelope out of his coat pocket, and opens it. Another white envelope. I can see that it is empty. In one hand he holds the envelope and with the other he lifts his thumb and forefinger to his head, then using them like a pair of tweezers he pulls out one strand of hair and slides it into the envelope, then another.

'One is never enough. I'll give you two, in case you lose one.'

The smile he gives me isn't an evil smile, it's a lonely one.

My previous encounter with the Cousin had occurred, almost auspiciously, shortly after Ivan bought his ticket to Minsk and left the country on an airplane, promising to return. The plant-filled apartment, the apartment that was meant to be ours, was practically in ruins; right up until my stay in hospital I lived in a room at Celeste's old place, which I shared with a number of other tenants. Mr Sirio, with his eastern dexterity, now managed and maintained—in a precious game of prices, exceptions, increases and discounts— every apartment in the building. Most of the tenants were students, but only a handful accepted my offers of maths and logic classes, and when they did it was inevitably the night before an exam, as a kind of last resort. I was patient, but I snapped pencils as I scrawled my explanations.

Once Ivan had gone to Minsk, there was nothing to do but immerse myself in my new role, perhaps sinking a little too deep, the way any other woman would have done. I bought magazines about cooking and magazines about natural living and fabrics, which I didn't even remove from their plastic wrapping. I had long conversations with the hairdresser about styles and ointments that might help tame my unruly mane, and left the salon laden with every possible chemical treatment, though my hair remained untouched. My efforts were hit and miss, a bit like Saturday night at the cinema.

For some time now the family had been going through a period of regeneration. As most of the cousins were now hitting forty, our aunts and uncles and ancestors from Las Flores and Junín and Buenos Aires were dropping like flies. We'd buried five of them over the past few years; then, less than a year ago, a sixth had died, smack bang in the middle of Ivan's absence. Ivan wasn't replying to any of my messages, and he'd only called once since his departure, using ancient landline technology. During the call we spoke anxiously about our trip through the desert, because it was the only thing we had in common; there was nothing to say about the present, aside from the same four unequivocal, unnecessary statements: over there it was freezing and snowing; here the air was boiling; we had to avoid making promises to each other; we were onto a good thing and loathe to lose it. The message, one month later, that flickered on my answering machine like a red star, the first I'd received in a long time, was not from Ivan but from a relative of mine who also lived in Buenos Aires. He announced that another family member—Aunt Berta this time—had died peacefully in her bed. The word *peacefully* was pronounced with great delight. This time the funeral would take place in Las Flores, where all present would dutifully have to praise the flowers in my mother's garden. What would I say to my sister? I would do my best not to look at the gumboots on her feet, the way she did every time she sat down.

I made my way to Las Flores, punctually. The wake was held in a funeral parlour filled with mothball-scented veils, in an unbearably hot room with fans milling indecisively above our heads. There he was, standing at the back as usual, studying the prey in his hunting grounds, because there were several of us now: mature, acceptable-looking, familiar. He came over and offered his condolences, and I did the same. When night fell he called in at my mother's house; we were baking and watching the snaggle-toothed anchors on the local Junín news channel. He came inside, ate a biscuit. Sure, why not, it might be nice to get some fresh air, take a walk around the town, which was a rare paradigm of constancy in this world. Little had changed, of course, so there was nothing to look at, and I tried to ignore the hands raised in recognition as we walked along.

I had nothing to talk to the Cousin about except Ivan, Minsk, the snow. But all the good things about Ivan and the snow seemed to have dissolved somehow, because several weeks had passed now, and Ivan had only thought to call me once in that time. Because I was a woman now, and spitefulness made sense to me, it was logical, and the Cousin nodded, stroking that new thin moustache of his.

When I walk into the kitchen, with the already eaten soup and the already washed dishes (I know I can't have been outside with the Cousin for more than twenty minutes), when I make my way back up the stairs, when I speak, I have to be someone new.

Mara didn't believe in love, or if she did it was only rarely, in winter, between five and six in the evening. It was all proven and documented—her meagre collection of bad poetry, her ardently expressed desires to play Juliet, or Melibea, in some theatre, or immediately, that very night—all could be traced to that precise hour on some cold winter's night. Afterwards, though, love left her.

In her shoebox that received no natural light and exhaled no vapours, Ludmila would nibble on rice crackers and sip on a thick juice that promised to feed her without anyone noticing. We spoke one more time after that night of the attempted threesome, which happened so shortly before her accident. She was perched on the edge of her seat like a flag on a flagpole, straight-backed and silent and splendid. She was good at pretending, and I was happy with her silence. If she'd thought to ask me, I would naturally have had to tell her the truth: that the night in question had been a kind of betrayal on her part, pure and simple. But she was discreet when she had to be, and it was much easier to stay quiet about that night with the Cousin, when the three of us had sat together in that same shoebox, in that very room. It's true: I had tried to undress in the bathroom, I had looked at myself topless in the mirror. My breasts had seemed like two errors, a millennium-old misunderstanding. I would have liked to walk out naked and say: This is nothing, you know, it's just a mammary gland with a slightly more sensitive bit on the end, surrounded by hair, and the skin covering it is coarse; Look! Look at this! Look at these little pimples, bring microscopes! But I'd already put my blouse back on, and shortly afterwards I'd returned home, to the apartment which, at that time, when I was twenty-two, was also Celeste's home.

On my last night with Ludmila we didn't talk about all that. Instead, she ranted about all those people in the world who didn't believe in authentic love—which is hard like a diamond but cannot be polished—and criticised the counterfeit love most people ended up settling for, the conformist love of long-established couples, of buyers of holidays and rings. We wandered out of the shoebox and into the street. We planned to spend every last cent of the night, as one does on last nights.

Ludmila was in love with a serious man this time, she told me as we got into the taxi. The man lived in Devoto, in a white house on a corner across the road from a plaza, where we stationed ourselves as inconspicuously as possible. Ludmila preferred married men, allegedly so as to avoid confusing romantic love with the love of families, or the love of domesticated animals. Her taste for married men wasn't a 'forbidden fruit' thing, she said.

One hour later, or two, the man left the house with a child and a dog.

'Let's go,' Ludmila said, and we followed him.

Then we stopped and waited for them to do another lap of the plaza, hoping they would see us. They didn't—the dog was old and tired quickly.

Then we went back into town and lost ourselves among the crowds at a house party, full of people feigning internationality; in reality there were only a handful of Spaniards there, and a single Colombian, who won hearts easily with his foreign accent and pendulous necklaces, squeezing us, confusing us, rubbing up against us.

I'm going to be someone new. No zombie blowflies from my past. The only thing I want now is to go back to Ivan, to the apartment that is mine, and Isaac's, the apartment that has been ours, mother and son's, for barely a few hours, since our return from the hospital. We played at the nativity scene earlier, and all three of us survived. The Cousin speaks to me from across the table, and the table is a barricade, and although it seems flat and horizontal it is actually vertical, and on the other side is an abyss.

'I have to go,' I repeat.

My insistence animates him, for a moment it almost beautifies him. His moustache no longer seems funny, the way it did in Las Flores, when we saw each other at the funeral.

Some other relative must have died in the last nine months, because the Cousin is making renewed calculations about new plots of land, never more than a half-hectare in size and no good for anything beyond a vegetable patch and a couple of pigs. His calculations are correct; the miserable rent such a plot would fetch, once divided between the nineteen or twenty cousins, scarcely seems worth the effort. (The number of cousins is as unstable as the number of ancestors who, like dead movie stars, live more fully in our memories than they ever did in life.)

'What's the rush?' he says to me now, positively glowing with pleasure. This time he doesn't restrain me; he stands up beside me and, like a hasty Casanova, leaves a small collection of bills on the table, which seems excessive for the single drink he ordered but in reality is insufficient. He is a great imposter, but the cheap dime-store kind, in spite of his moustache, which he smooths down the way he used to smooth his long fringe. He exhales a kind of noble cynicism. But it's as if he's gone soft inside—perhaps he even has feelings.

'I can see you're not going to let me meet the kid, and that's wrong, you're wrong. But you know what? It kinda suits you, this whole thing.'

Back on the footpath he whispers into my ear for a while, because he's convinced that sooner or later I'll change my mind.

'I'm with Ivan now.' This is all I can give him in response.

'Wrong again. You're with me.'

He knows how to be literal when it suits him.

'That's true.'

He grabs me, bends my face towards his, and stamps a bright imprint deep into my cheek. I half-jog across the street, the way any woman would do, and if it weren't for the hospital perhaps I would run.

'Don't forget to test it!' he yells when I reach the other side. He makes pathetic signs at me, as if waving from the coastline at a great ship that is sailing away.

It must have happened like this, out of urgency: you learn that your friend has died the most pointless of deaths, crushed in the traffic of some city; you get angry, you get sad; you squeeze your eyes first, because they're capsizing, then your chest. Suddenly, with a fist in your chest, you no longer feel anything. You are no longer being pulled by some magnet, nothing attracts you or repels you. You are a mute piece of wood. You feel relieved.

But Mara refused to believe me, back then. She made up some fight that had never existed, over some man who wasn't worth the two steps it would take to clear a passage for him to walk in the door. We were very young, and Mara was ashamed of her tears, which came out of her so round and large. Just a week ago, the three of us had sworn never to cry for more than ten seconds each month. We were breaking all our oaths.

She cried for a long time that day, improvising all kinds of chords, like a solitary instrument, and she couldn't bear for me to leave her alone.

'It's because of that guy, because she took him from you.'

There in the large kitchen of Celeste's apartment, where we'd sought refuge after learning of Ludmila's accident, Mara had turned dramatically, as if she were wearing a long cape and there were a strong breeze blowing in her face, exhorting her tears.

'Are you sad or not?'

'I'm sad.'

'Did you love her as much as I did?'

'I can't possibly know the answer to that.'

She kept turning and turning. Then she dragged me out into the street, rebuking the driver of every car she saw, until we stopped out the front of the shoebox where Ludmila had lived. We embarked then on a pilgrimage, stopping first at the shoe shop where Ludmila had worked, then on and on to several more stations. Then it was time for me to leave her. But she refused. If we stayed together, Ludmila wasn't really dead, she said, and other illogical things of that nature. She begged me not to go home, folding her hands in supplication and spitting her words at me. Then she asked me how I managed to keep myself together, what hidden thing was I holding onto to maintain my sanity?

'It's a ball,' I replied.

'Your sanity is a ball? I don't believe that.'

'You have to squeeze the pit of your stomach.'

We said goodbye. I was working as a maths teacher back then, in an after-school program, and I spent the afternoons breaking chalk against blackboards.

I'm back. I have trouble with the door again, the mischievous key. I go back up the granite stairs. I think: Ivan will be watching me, he'll be worried, because I've been gone almost half an hour. I'm sure I'll end up telling him the truth; I'll get down on my knees if I have to. It's significant, I think, this question of *intention*. I look up, and see that there is nobody standing at the top of the stairs. I continue. In my pocket I have an envelope that weighs a tonne against my thigh. I look into the kitchen, but there is nobody there. I look down the plant-filled hallway, but there is nobody there either. The floor seems made of mud; I have to navigate my way through carefully. I take a few steps down the hallway and bump into something; I stop. I stoop down to pick it up: it's a cardboard box. I retreat a few steps until the kitchen light illuminates it: it says *Bagley* on it, which is the name of a biscuit brand. This triggers something in me, but I stay perfectly still.

The night of Aunt Berta's funeral in Las Flores, I went out for a walk with the Cousin, around the town that so resembled itself, and we talked about Ivan, who had disappeared in Minsk, and my spite, which was a new insect in my collection. We studied it together, like scientists. The Cousin was so proud of his thin, black, perky moustache. He took me to a house I'd never been inside, although I recognised everyone who lived there, and they each greeted me with a kiss as though they knew me and remembered my name. Then, of course, we had to sit down and drink *yerba mate* and eat bread and fried pork rinds, despite the late hour and our indigestion. On the television someone was talking about distant wars, then the weather forecast for Buenos Aires. We also played cards. Another cousin arrived, then two women wearing tight, ill-fitting jeans that struggled to contain their thighs and buttocks.

'I've got a nice room upstairs with music and everything. It's a really simple set-up—when you're in the country, you know, you don't want to come across as a show-off.'

It seemed strange to me that, despite all those plots of land he'd acquired off the other cousins and the surviving uncles and aunts, all he had to show for himself was a room on a neighbour's roof terrace. I told him this.

'I don't want to be a show-off,' he repeated.

It was the first time I'd seen him tell a bad lie, and I could see now that he was aging—more quickly, perhaps, than he should have. The curtain in his room had been pegged to the wall with thumbtacks. The celebrated music set-up dated to before the turn of the century. After a lot of fiddling around he managed to turn it on, and we were met with the relentless fuzz of radio snow, which couldn't be silenced even with a cassette, because the cassette player had apparently stopped working that same day. Just a few hours ago, he insisted.

'How long has it been since we saw each other?'

'Four years,' I answered, and sat down.

'We're not the same,' he said, and I agreed.

'Look at this.'

He handed me two engraved glasses filled with liquor, which I drank. Together we figured out which family must have sent it, and this filled us with a childish, leisurely joy. It was good, surrendering ourselves to what was easy and familiar, to the two or three drops of blood we shared in common, in that shortcut of a town that was once my home. The Cousin had apparently suffered some kind of misfortune, and now it seemed he vaguely believed in feelings; I knew this because it took us a long time to get into bed, and as long again to get into sex, and before we did we had to spend hours weaving genealogies between the grid-like streets of the town, and confessing the deterioration of our skin and our breath, which also ages.

Towards the end there was even a half-hearted attempt to arrange another meeting, something that hadn't happened once in the twenty years we'd known each other. The spite I felt towards Ivan wasn't quite great enough to allow that, but I was proud of it nevertheless, proud to feel abandoned by a man at last.

Our conversation was so sickly sweet that a paper lantern hanging from the ceiling transformed, slowly, into a moon. At five in the morning we got dressed, and at six we watched the flat, clear rural sunrise, without a single cloud to obstruct or colour it.

'Last time I saw you, you were with a professor. Did you dump him? I'm with a nurse now, she likes instruments.'

'He left, he went to live overseas.'

'How much longer did you stay together?'

It was enough to keep walking and kicking up dust to keep the conversation alive.

'The night you turned up and gave me the calculator— that's the night we split up.'

'What an honour. Was there a lot of crying and swearing?'

As the daylight increased, so did the level of sarcasm. We had breakfast at the bus station, amid other people's bags, mimicking a farewell that never took place. I went back to my mother's house for a few more days, and he went back to his room on the roof terrace.

The night Pedro and I broke up, the cat escaped under the washing machine and into the tree while Pedro and I regretted not going to Tigre. We sat there on the balcony, our bowls of tomato soup eaten, inventing hypotheses about the terrible smell that wafted to us from some indistinct place, from the port or the city. We'd promised never to invest in wineglasses, or a car, or jealous thoughts, but the night itself invited exceptions to all our rules; the smell in the air, the prowling cat, the hours accumulating too quickly on the clock face, all of it seemed to portend transgression.

'Did you ever love him?'

'The cousin? No, I never loved him.'

'Are you telling me the truth?'

'I always tell you the truth.'

Perhaps he even made an effort to stay seated, to maintain that masculine, erudite voice of his, rounded with so many insights. All he needed was a pipe, but he'd never smoked—the ever-looming question of mortality warned him against it.

'But I saw you kissing him. Why did you kiss him?'

'Because he asked me to.'

'And if I asked you to stand up, step over this railing and throw yourself off the balcony?'

And so began the arguments. Soon we would be two theologians discussing the sex of angels.

'And me? Did you love me?' he ventured. It was a dangerous path, and a well-conjugated verb.

'Yes, I loved you.'

'But it wasn't *love*.'

'I thought you didn't care about love,' I replied.

Pedro reached down to scratch his foot.

'How could I not care about love?'

'No,' I said, plainly. 'It wasn't love, but I'm trying, and I'm getting better, I'm better. Can't you see I'm getting better?'

I was starting to get desperate.

'Better? What, because you can make rice? Because you can brush a cat?'

It was as though, when he reached down to scratch his foot, Pedro's hands had unearthed the rough stone of scepticism, and now he set to polishing it at length, casting its lustre over everything that was ours. Ah, he said, in surprise, because scepticism is refreshing, and he must have felt invigorated by it.

It was true: over the past few days I'd been revelling in simple tasks like brushing the cat, choosing names for it, baking a cake, feeling excitement over the whipped cream I could hide inside it.

I left Pedro on the balcony and went to the kitchen to wash the soup bowls, and sweep up the crumbs on the table. I wanted to be better, I wanted to correct myself. You pick up a plate and you put it in its place, and automatically you're a better person. But the dishes had all been washed and put away by Pedro while I was downstairs with the Cousin. I needed some numbers, so I got out an old set of scales someone had bequeathed to us and started weighing whatever we had in the pantry: sugar, lentils, flour, anything I could find that was clear and unmistakable, and in my head I added up the beautiful combinations of numbers. Pedro returned from the balcony as though from the North Pole, his face clean and red and gaping.

'43, 86,' I said to him, and the sentence was perfectly balanced.

'What's that?'

Pedro had never accused me with a question like that before.

'*Smoke* and *the balcony*. In the lottery. With Celeste, when…'

But there was nowhere to go with such vividness. Pedro sat down at the kitchen table, spread open his green book, right in the middle, like a map, and started to read. For a while now the cat had been pushing a plastic bottle cap around the kitchen.

I should have left, but I'd decided a few days earlier that I wanted to be a woman. I wanted to stay, at any cost, as long as I could afford to. I was even prepared to practice the strange gymnastics of self-sacrifice, if necessary—to flex my voluptuous female imagination, to believe in tragedies, like believing in a storm before the afternoon has yet turned black. The cat jumped onto the kitchen bench and knocked over a jar of sugar, which smashed. I picked up the pieces of glass. The cat had nails like a parrot, and as it fled they made a sound like chimes. The cat disappeared through the door and returned moments later with a piece of string.

Pedro was reading. I tried to get some fresh air through the bedroom window, but the air there was the same, rancid and burnt. I went back to the kitchen. I'm not sure what the cat did to deserve it, but as I walked in Pedro gave the animal a kick that sent it flying. Next to the pantry I saw the Bagley biscuits box the cat had arrived in, three days earlier. I picked up the box and placed it on the table. Then I grabbed the cat by the scruff of the neck and placed it inside, squirming. I closed the box. Without releasing my grip I leaned down, picked up the string, and tied it around the box. First I made a simple knot, then I elaborated on it. I sat down and asked Pedro to sit next to me. The box sat on the table between us, like a bottle of wine between two lovers, embellishing us, in a way, with its shadow. I got up to fetch a knife. Pedro stood up abruptly, tipping over his chair, and took two steps backwards. I should have laughed, I should have reassured him that it wasn't what it looked like.

I lifted the knife and stabbed it into the cardboard box.

'What are you doing?'

'It's so it can breathe.'

'Don't do that!' Pedro screamed.

He didn't understand that it was just so the cat could breathe better.

Scepticism is the first thing to die, the women used to say. It's a kind of magic spell lonely men use; it helps them open their mouths in the day and close their eyes at night. But then along comes a child, or a brother, or a sick person, and suddenly the men are cured.

I did return from Las Flores, and Ivan did return from Minsk; he travelled at least twenty thousand kilometres, I two hundred. The minute we saw each other all was forgiven—it was a kind of pre-emptive forgiveness, since neither really knew what we were forgiving. Ah, but forgiveness is nefarious; there is more than one gold tooth hiding there, inside its mouth.

Soon afterwards I discovered that *human nature*—something I'd presumed to be long dead, or at least in its death throes—had knocked at the door, and my body, against all odds, had answered. The blood test proved it. Ivan had gone to pick up the results, and now he brandished them before me. It was a Tuesday and, therefore, a good day for making errors, or for fearing them.

'You're pregnant.'

I asked him to say it to me in Russian, and he obliged with a musical refrain.

Ivan was a doctor, he had the blood tests in his hand, there was no doubt about it.

'Do you want to keep it?'

'Whatever you say,' I replied, without a trace of submissiveness. It was a reply born of pure realism: whatever he said about the future always happened, and whatever he said about the present was always true. I'd had only a few weeks to verify this—two or three weeks wedged between our trip through the desert and his departure for Minsk— but already it seemed to be an immutable fact.

After three months he'd returned, and we'd forgiven one another without delay. For a while we lived together in the ugly rooming house he was staying in while he fixed up the apartment. He tolerated that place, with its flimsy partition walls separating the rooms, because he was used to austerity, and because it was cheap, and he needed to save, in case Minsk called him back, in case war returned. I'd told him there wouldn't be a war here for several years, but who knew if I or something like me was even capable of keeping him in Buenos Aires for long.

I was being cautious, I was simply answering his question. How we'd laughed, Mara and I, at the wolfish women, all those years ago; and now here I was, carnivorous at last, and circling my prey.

'I can get rid of it, if you want,' he said.

'Whatever you say. What you say is all that matters.'

We didn't broach the topic again for a few days. Then:

'I'm not getting rid of it, we're keeping it.'

'OK,' I replied. The whole thing was frighteningly easy.

We were lying on our backs in bed. The bedroom lights were out and only the neighbour's light remained, along with his music: a bastardised, mellifluous sound we'd also grown used to.

'We're going to be together. You're good, I'm good.'

It was all very easy. I said yes.

'I'm going to work better, as a doctor. You too. And you'll always tell the truth. And I'll always tell the truth.'

'Are you going to take me to Minsk?'

'It's cold, bad weather.'

'To the desert, then?'

'Back to the desert, yes, like in the summer.'

What a sky, we said or didn't say as we got out of the car. It was still early, and the sky had that peculiar whiteness it gets before an afternoon of unbearable heat. After singing its complaints to us the motor had overheated, which it shouldn't have; that is, the mechanic from Avenida Warnes hadn't anticipated it happening.

I didn't know how much Ivan knew, we'd only just met, but then he popped the bonnet and I thought: he knows. We were in the middle of the desert, and the phone we'd brought with us was picking up no signals. Half an hour passed, and not a single car went by. Ivan removed his head from underneath the chassis and said:

'I don't know.'

We were at kilometre 186, about halfway to our destination. Ivan handed me my backpack and pointed to the opposite side of the road. I obeyed. We looked at each other for a while, face to face with the black highway between us, but it was a sad spectacle, with nothing to shade us from the sun, and we eventually succumbed to surviving as best we could, each in our own way. Then a green car passed, but it didn't stop, then a blue one, which didn't stop either. A third car did stop, about twenty metres from where I was standing, and there was no time to say goodbye or make an agreement about what would happen next. When I opened the car door a couple was arguing inside. They went quiet the minute I sat down. Since there was nowhere to go but the end of the road, and I knew nothing about what might have gone wrong with the car, there wasn't much to talk about. They busied themselves with the air conditioner. After glancing at me twice in the rear-view mirror, the woman asked me to please not touch the seats, if my hands were dirty, nor to touch the sleeping child who, I now realised, was sitting beside me in the back seat. The child was resting in his plastic capsule like a placid alien in his spaceship. I told her it would never have crossed my mind to touch either the seat or the child. She didn't seem satisfied with my response, and her worried glances persisted in the crooked rectangle of the mirror. The drive took around forty minutes, and it was almost three o'clock when we arrived at the intersection where the highway ended. The desert hotel loomed before us. They wished me luck, the way one might farewell a recently convicted prisoner, and I stepped out into the heat. I walked the sparsely gravelled path to the hotel and went inside. The hotel was a 1970s style building, pug-nosed and spacious; in the middle of the foyer, the man at the reception desk sat chewing on a toothpick. The landline was touch and go, he explained, so best try with the phone I had. I might have better luck up on that little hill, he suggested, pointing outside. He'd heard there was an antenna to the north somewhere, but he'd never seen it; he always tried on the Neuquén side.

One minute longer and I'm sure he would have given me his name, his role (which he performed badly), and every nickname he'd ever been given, behind which he disguised, chameleon-like, the many miseries of his existence.

I walked back outside and ascended the rocky hill he'd suggested. When I arranged my arm and torso in a very specific position, I got a signal. The emergency number rang out; it was January. I went back to the hotel. The man at reception wrote another number for me on a scrap of paper. An old dog was sleeping on her side by the edge of the path in a sliver of shade, her black teats hanging like fruit. I climbed back up the hill and assumed the position. This time I spoke to an unhelpful woman who claimed to be 'just an employee'—apparently everyone else at the towing company was asleep, taking the afternoon siesta. I asked her for details she couldn't give me; nobody would be back in the office until five or six in the evening, she said. I'd have to call back then. I convinced her to take a message: Grey car, numberplate unknown. Driver's name Ivan. No, no surname. Which kilometre? Kilometre 186—of this, at least, I was certain. Urgent towing required.

Yes, the woman said, it's quite hot out.

Could she guarantee me someone would head out there this evening?

She asked me to repeat the kilometre.

Then the conversation ended, with no way of retrieving it.

I was carrying my backpack, and there was a hotel with ceiling fans standing just a few metres away.

I walked to the intersection. A line of ants was making a pilgrimage towards a dead creature on the highway. I couldn't see a single car coming from either the north or the south. There was nobody returning from the desert, either, who might turn at the intersection and take me up towards Mendoza, where a dubious aunt of Mara's was meant to be waiting for me. It was half past three. My head was so hot it seemed to burn of its own free will. I was at kilometre 285; I started to backtrack on foot, and the wolf in my heart howled with excitement.

'50!' Celeste would yell from her bedroom, not long after waking. I'm sure she would have liked me to run, but I took my time delivering her second piece of bread for the morning.

'36!'

And I would bring her a knob of butter, which she would often reject with a shake of her finger, as if she'd lost her voice, even though she'd just spoken to me a moment before. At such times I understood that number 36 was not being used as a code; Celeste was requesting the thing she'd been requesting ever since I arrived from Las Flores at the age of fifteen or sixteen, like so many other visiting relatives, and moved in with her. I would return to the apartment, from school or work, and the minute I opened the door Celeste would yell a number at me, and I would have to walk straight back out and close the door behind me and go downstairs to complete my mission. The lottery tickets were sold just down the road, from a little hole-in-the-wall teethed with metal bars. Celeste was on a first-name basis with every employee. She would give them that week's number, along with the number of pesos she wanted to bet on it, which never changed. But they would always ask:

Ten?

Ten.

On number 36.

On the 24th.

Which was the day of the draw, if she was playing a few days in advance.

Everything has just happened. I've just gone downstairs, just seen the Cousin, just received the rancid kiss he stamped on my cheek, deep into my flesh. I've just come back up the stairs. I've just walked down the hallway and bumped into a cardboard box. *Oncemore* it's a Bagley biscuits box. *Oncemore* it's night. I lift my nose, thinking of that other night, the night Pedro and I separated. I tell myself it's impossible. But it *is* possible. We ate red soup that night, too, and the air again tastes burnt, and I re-imagine that it must be a boat down at the port, some kind of chemical spill, but this time the thought isn't soothing at all. I look into the bedroom; the baby isn't there, nor is Ivan. I look into the other bedroom, and see a lonely light.

Maternity equals contingency: one must surrender to it, embrace it.

That night of our separation we sat across from one another, with the table and the box between us, which moved less and less and seemed less and less like a decoration, less and less like a bottle of wine or a lover's bouquet. Pedro had made me stop stabbing the knife into it, so there were very few breathing holes. We looked at one another over the box, our hands were shaking now.

'What do you want me to do with the box?' he asked. He seemed composed.

'I just put it in the box so you could take it.'

'Where am I supposed to take it at this hour? I don't know what happened. You were so happy, you spent all afternoon brushing it.'

'It was wrong. It was a subterfuge.'

'The cat, or what you did?'

'Both.'

Logic: it soon fades, and nobody mourns it.

Pedro left with the box. He was gone for two hours. The smell in the air hadn't dissipated by the time I went to bed. I even went to the trouble of brushing my teeth beforehand. He returned at four in the morning and sat on the bed with his shoes on, crossing his legs like an Indian sage, and told me a job had come up at an overseas university. He wasn't sure it he was completely interested in it (we had always been suspicious of the *incompleteness* of things) but he had a feeling it could be his—if only ideologically, or politically, or specifically. He'd applied for the overseas job without telling me, earlier that week. If he got it, he would leave immediately.

He got up and put on his coat.

He told me he was going to Tigre, which was impossible at such an early hour, unless he planned on walking there. At least thirty kilometres separated us from the delta and the islands within it. Perhaps if he ran, at a good pace, he might be able to make the eight o'clock ferry.

If there was ever any love between us it had died, like an animal.

Those women, chewing on the tips of their spoons and biros in agony, were stuck between the *right* to have a child and the *duty* to have a child. They formed long queues at the clinics of psychoanalysts and pedicurists.

I must have faith. The angel of contingency must be suspended from some building, somewhere in the city. This night is just another night. History doesn't have to repeat itself. I still have the Bagley biscuits box in my hand, which is not good. I take it into the kitchen. I prefer not to put it on the floor so I put in on the table, then I go back into the hallway. I take a few steps. I don't hear anything until I'm almost at the bottom of the spiral staircase that leads up to the roof terrace. I hesitate; I can hear the baby speaking in the only primitive language he knows, and his voice is piercing.

Could he be alone up there?

No—now I hear Ivan answering him. It all seems so much easier in Russian; to console, to apologise, to forgive. I lose faith; I remove my foot from the bottom stair.

But, what is this? There is no blowfly here, I think, and I hit my head against the wall. I run upstairs.

The two of them are in the middle of the terrace, making one shape. I walk towards them, but I keep my distance; my heart is still and serious, like quartz covered in black points.

'He was on the ground. The cot collapsed.'

'Really?'

A bubbling thing throbs in my fingers. It must be desperation. But it's best not to get too close; there is a Bagley biscuits box downstairs, waiting. And the wind that blows up here is rancid. I have to refrain from whatever it is, until tomorrow.

'His bottle was full, didn't you give him anything?'

He almost doesn't inflect the question, because he doesn't expect anything from me, but I defend myself:

'I tried and I couldn't, he didn't want any.'

Ivan laughs, like he was lifting a sword. The white envelope burns through my pocket to my thigh. I make a weak
attempt at saying something sensible. Then I start to ramble,
and my tongue rolls miserably in my mouth, so I go quiet
and follow the two of them up and down the terrace. The
gentle pacing is meant to find silence, to clean away the fright
and the pain of the fallen cot. All I have to do is watch them,
I realise. If I follow their steps, the blood flows properly
again. They walk into the flooded tool shed, they walk out
again, they go back down the stairs. We've been going up
and down those stairs all night, ever since I came home from
the hospital, ever since *we* came home, and it seems we will
have to continue. Until recently I believed that this novel
kind of exertion, this enthusiasm, was of very little value. I
follow them downstairs and apologise. I say let's go back up,
let's keep going, no, don't go into the kitchen.

Ivan doesn't hear me, though he is right not to. Ivan is
always right. The baby is crying again, and for an instant
Ivan loses his patience; he puts him down in one of the
kitchen chairs, then another; there is something sitting in a
pot on the stove, he is boiling medals and ribbons and other
Soviet trivia that he wants to rescue, in this unusual manner, and he can't manage it with the baby in his arms. It's
impossible, it's too dangerous, he tells himself, but instead
of handing the baby to me he leaves him in a chair. He is
about to put the baby inside the Bagley biscuits box but he
changes his mind at the last minute and props him up in
the chair. I watch from the doorway, directly beneath the
lintel. Going in would be a mistake; not going in would
also be a mistake. The baby shifts, and so does the flimsy
chair he's been left in.

When the thinking men got together, things followed a certain routine. Over the first couple of drinks they would talk about football, as if condescending to the rest of the world. If there were no women present, they would talk about women. Then they would switch to politics, which they would discuss at length—this was the one rope they refused to release.

During my year with Pedro, I would sometimes leave the refuge of the bedroom and watch the men from the doorway, standing beneath the lintel. I would observe their trousers and their scuffed shoes, the way they stroked their beards. I had memorised several of the names they often liked to recite, like priests in a temple, and when I got the chance—for instance, when I delivered them another bottle of whatever they were drinking—I would say some of the names out loud, as a kind of friendly gesture. If someone said Kojève, he got to sit in one of the armchairs; if someone said Kant, he received a glass of something, or a snack. Those who were not yet acquainted would measure each other up, listing grants won and positions held, before beginning on the familiar task of replaying old phrases and old ideas, all disguised and dressed up to various degrees, throwing out sentences the way they'd earlier thrown out names, sentences like: *The instinct of the animal is oriented to survival*; *Knowledge is located at the limits of knowledge*; and other such remixes of words pronounced four or twenty-four centuries ago, now duly refurbished, polished, and spat into new cocoons.

Pedro had his favourite catchphrase, which he made sure to pronounce at a point in the night when he was certain it would not go unnoticed. If someone knocked over a glass for the second time, if someone sneezed more than once, he couldn't help himself. One night, red in the cheeks, he asked me to come in and close a window I'd already closed, hours earlier. This happened at least twice. Then, pointing that long finger of irony I'd never been able to comprehend, with that special wink of complicity that united them, when I came in *oncemore* to deliver a bottle of wine, or to fulfil his unnecessary request and close the innocuous and already closed window, he would pronounce: *There is no such thing as an isolated incident; One time is no time.* And then, as if someone had let a cat into a birdcage, a great ruckus would ensue, and other phrases would flutter in the air like fallen feathers.

I fear it might be true. There is a reincarnation hidden in the toppled salt shaker.

When you look in the mirror it is opaque, it looks dirty and worm-eaten, or your own face inverted in the glass is a kind of joke. But the salt shaker falls, again and again; life is composed of a finite number of events.

It's true: after the wedding where I first met the Cousin there was another wedding, years later, where we saw each other again. After the meal with the rich neighbours in Tigre there was another meal, in the same gazebo, three years later, when one of the women saw me at the port and insisted on dragging me into a boat, when Ivan already existed and I barely did, when he was in Minsk and I spent my weekends wandering like a ghost between old and new places.

There were two kids named Matías.

But these are all spurious repetitions, they might even make me laugh if Pedro still existed, if I could touch his arm and say: That greasy little catchphrase of yours, the one you think makes you a *thinking man*, the one I mistrusted so intensely out of love for that other music, the perfect music of numbers; that catchphrase finally came true.

The Bagley biscuits box is still sitting on the table. Ivan has his back to me, but since the back of his head can see and speak I don't move a muscle. Isaac stretches up his arms from the bottom of the bottomless chair. I tell myself: it's time for you to go in there and take him off that chair. But I can't. It's time for you to go to the bathroom, then, and wash your face—that is, if anything even remains between your hairline and the crease of your neck; your eyes, especially, so you can think better. I crouch down, I keep myself like a secret, I wait one more minute.

It happened again. In big families, just as there is an endless stream of deaths, there is an endless stream of young people who are more or less alive and decide to make a public event of getting married, at which event women are forced to wear dresses and everyone present is forced to get drunk. In the year of Pedro, at the very beginning of that year, it happened again. It was *oncemore* a rented venue with a cheap castle façade, and walls of imitation stone manufactured from some depressing material. I walked in and *oncemore* I chose a table at the back, although this time I wasn't dragging Celeste along because Celeste had died not long before. Also seated at my table were a mother and a teenage daughter, not from Las Flores, who were silently competing, with their low-cut dresses and feminine wiles, for the Cousin's attention. When he saw me he threaded his long, graceful body towards me through the crowd of grotesque human bodies on the dance floor. He took a seat between the mother and daughter and fiddled with his cigarette in the ashtray. All of this had already happened, several years ago. Just as we'd done that other night, we hung around until the last of the stragglers finally threw in the towel—until both mother and daughter started yawning and the waiters refused to serve us any more drinks. Then, like last time, only without Celeste between us to chaperone, we left the party and got into a taxi. I was low maintenance, he told me. I never turned up with a meddlesome plus one, I didn't need gifts and flowers, and I didn't cry over soppy love songs.

Twice Mara vanished into anonymity; first after Ludmila's death, then again on the brink of giving birth.

Celeste fell out of bed two times; each time she broke a different bone.

Now I'm in the kitchen. Ivan has just left without looking at me. It's very simple, I just have to arrange the baby inside, so I do. I close the box.

Ivan returns with a pile of old Russian newspapers and I think, with an unfamiliar sense of melodrama, that this is the end of days, and at the end of days newspapers and clocks and promises serve no purpose at all. This thought is a relief.

'I lied to you,' I say as Ivan props the pile of newspapers on the kitchen bench. He starts to sort through them.

'Where's Isaac?' he asks.

'Here,' I reply. I take a knife. I stab it once into the cardboard box on the table beneath me. The box betrays me; it moves. Ivan doesn't turn around, so he doesn't notice. I realise I was wrong to believe the back of his head could see and hear and speak, like the face of a benevolent monster.

'I was with someone, when you left. But only because I loved you,' I say, and the inconsistency of that sentence, the baseness of it, the black hole it dissolves into makes me feel ashamed—now, at this moment, I feel myself falling and I have to hold out my hand, and I let go of the box, and the box betrays me again and starts to speak.

There was another catchphrase Pedro used to repeat, which he claimed was his by virtue of inheritance: *In order not to lie, one must lie to oneself.* This despite his being a committed sociologist, despite the fat green books that grew like plants all over the kitchen and the tiny bedroom we had to sleep in. There was no doubt that, with time, Pedro had acquired a certain taste for the scepticism of his esteemed colleagues and acquaintances, experts in theories of language and the impossibilities of language, and together they travelled towards that paradoxical place, happy in their impotence.

Mara used to tell me it was easy. She said I should try it. Rotating like a planet around her nine-months-pregnant belly, she showed me how. It usually happened when she was experiencing one of her fears, those fears she hoarded with the fervour of a coin collector, or when she was sure something bad was about to happen. She would choose a place—Oslo, say, or the outskirts of Istanbul—then she would choose a *good* character and a *good* role, and she would repeat the adjective to me several times in different pitches, as if warming up her voice: *goooood, guuuoooooood.* For the exercise to work, both had to be fundamentally and undeniably *good.* Then, all that was left was to find the right positioning of the body, then flick or tie back the hair, then say the lines. She'd played El Cid for a long time after that guy she'd met at the concert left her; she'd played Dido for a while after finding out about the loss of her first baby. Yes, she told me, you were there and you didn't even realise. We were sitting there on the couch together talking about the woman with all the necklaces, but in fact I wasn't talking about that at all—I was Dido when I said 'All those red beads.'

And what about those nights? I wanted to know after she confessed. Where had she been all those nights of mourning, as the other women drank beer and ranted about men and shoes and said *the damsel* and *the phallus*?

In Berlin, as a punk, and in Budapest, with her heart divided between the two halves of the city.

I try it now, because I need it now more than ever. The box is alive.

I say aloud to the back of Ivan's head: Ivan, we're in the desert. We've just saved each other in the middle of the desert. I you, you me. It's so hot, we should open a window.

The only two cars that passed me during the first hour of my walk along the highway were headed in the opposite direction, towards the desert hotel I'd come from. One stopped. The driver wound down his window and asked me what I was doing all alone in the forty-degree heat.

'I'm going to kilometre 186.'

'But there's nothing there.'

He meant no service station, no ranch.

A moment later he wound the window back up—he was wasting precious air conditioning—and nodded goodbye. It made sense; all around me glowed an aura of absurdity. I continued walking for a long while, surprised by those pools of water that always seem to form in the distance of deserts but are always an illusion. The fact that the water was an illusion didn't stop me from seeing it; in fact, I saw it precisely *because* it was an illusion. One hour later a yellow truck with a long trailer passed me, heading in the right direction, then an orange truck, which finally stopped many metres away and honked its horn to make me hurry up. I broke into a jog; the truck wouldn't wait forever, after all. The passenger door opened. I told the driver about the car, about Ivan, I told him how many hours Ivan had been waiting alone in the middle of the desert—about three, according to my calculations. The driver didn't care, and signalled for me to get in. Only then did I realise that he already had a passenger: a sandal-clad, tree-fingered teenager who didn't bat an eyelid as I jumped up beside him. We drove on. At kilometre 195 I could already see there was nothing waiting for us at kilometre 186.

'Are you sure?' the driver asked when I told him to stop anyway. 'You must have got the number wrong.'

I got out and sat on the edge of the ragged bitumen, resting my hot feet against the hot gravel that marked the beginning of the desert. It was five o'clock, there was no way the tow truck could have already come and gone. But there was no car here, and no Ivan; I couldn't even see the empty container of motor oil we'd found discarded next to a bush and left there, untouched. I waited until the clock read six-thirty, although the sky and the unremitting sun seemed to refute it.

The next vehicle to stop was a van. The man inside refrained from asking me what I was doing alone in the middle of the highway. I had used all the water to douse my head, and I was thirsty. I made the most of the silence and closed my eyes for a while.

The spell of the warm air washing through the windows abruptly broke when we arrived at the tiny hamlet of La Reforma. I pushed open the van door and extended a hand blackened by dust to the driver. I crossed a bone-dry square that seemed to serve as both a plaza and the entrance to the town. On the other side of it loomed a service station. There were dogs standing against every wall.

The service station employee conceded that several grey cars had passed since that morning, but he hadn't seen any tow trucks, empty or full.

I went back outside; one of the dogs looked dead. In the whole hamlet, which extended for just three blocks, there was only one grocery store, and inside it I found a single public telephone. I'd decided to call Mara in Buenos Aires—maybe she'd heard from Ivan. It was a futile hope, born of sunstroke. The store and the service station survived off the meagre rewards hurled to them from the bitumen: the occasional harried traveller, hungry for petrol or dinner. Inside the grocery store there were only five products, distributed unaesthetically across the shelves, and some wrinkled cold meats inside a tall refrigerator. All the heads inside the store were turned like sunflowers to the television, but when I entered they rotated towards me. I mustn't have looked like a promising customer, because a moment later they all turned their eyes back to the tyranny of the screen, in perfect silence.

I walked over to the telephone and put some coins inside it, which were promptly spat back out. I went to the counter, where two women were standing inspecting their nails. I held out a considerable sum of money and asked if there was a working telephone I could use. One of the women took the money and signalled for me to follow her.

We left the shop and walked two blocks, past a burning shed with a half-dismantled car inside it, and entered a small house. There was a telephone sitting on a nightstand; the line crackled, and Mara didn't answer. Perhaps she'd decided to bring her son into the world that very afternoon.

'Can't get onto him?' the woman asked.

She told me that, even though this was a small town, she'd seen her fair share of trouble; I wasn't the first woman to be discarded here, left by the side of the road like an abandoned dog, and I wouldn't be the last.

'The room costs two hundred pesos, including a *yerba mate* for breakfast.'

'I'll give you the same amount if you take me back to the highway.'

'What do you expect to find out there?' she answered. But if I had the money and I wanted to throw it away, by all means. One of her sons, who was young and named Matías, would take me later, in the ute. She made it very clear that when I came back I would not be welcome to stay the night—she went to bed early, and she wasn't going to get up in the middle of the night to prepare my room.

I told her I wouldn't be coming back. She concluded, with some sadness, that I was a fool and a dreamer.

Ivan refuses to play along. We're not in the desert, he says. He won't open the window, although he isn't afraid of the cold—it's not for his sake but for Isaac's that he refuses to open the window, because Isaac is only a month and a bit old, and a draught of cool air could cause him breathing difficulties, or activate some virus, or trigger a fever. Ivan still won't turn around. He removes the medals and ribbons from the pot like crabs and noodles.

From the passenger seat of the ute I could see the setting sun, the elaborate plays of light and artifice unfolding on the horizon. We passed kilometre 186 once on the way up, then again on the way back, then once more. There was nothing there. The kid called Matías wanted to know if maybe I'd gotten the number wrong. I said no. Was it before or after the firebreak? I'd never seen a firebreak in my life.

That's it there, he said, pointing. Stretching like a belt across the plain of desert was an even more lifeless strip of land, designed to stop fires from spreading.

Matías was very young, and realised too late that we'd run out of petrol. We puttered to an abandoned ranch and stole a few litres. We cut open a plastic bottle and funnelled as much as we could to the ute, spilling it on our hands and clothes in the process.

When we returned to kilometre 186 I told Matías to stop and let me out.

Overhead there was a lovers' sky, deep red, which I only discovered when I lifted my head.

The kid held the door open for me, puzzled. But because he was young, and there was barely enough petrol in the tank to fuel the drive back to La Reforma, and some girl was no doubt waiting for him there, sweating into some mattress, he finally nodded, closed the door, and left me. Night was falling.

I sat down beside the metal sign that said 186. The sign was riddled with bullet holes—the result of poor marksmanship, or the frustration of poachers.

'Where's Isaac?' Ivan asks me now. Finally, he turns around. He thinks he's overcome the feeling of mistrust he felt towards me; he doesn't realise he's about to discover an even greater motive for it.

I look at the box. For the last little while I've been stabbing the knife into it on all sides, to let the air in.

Ivan runs at me, knocks me aside—I fall to the ground.

He throws the knife from the table, opens the box, and rescues Isaac from inside.

He breathes air into the baby's mouth.

Now he's holding him. Now he's walking out, he's running down the hallway until he is lost in the darkness. But no; the lost one is me.

I get up to follow him. I find the two of them in the bedroom with the fallen cot. I observe the resuscitation in silence; it only takes a moment. I'm still standing. No thoughts are in my head, and this surprises me.

Now Ivan starts to clean him, he has taken some washcloths out of a new box, one I haven't seen before, along with some lotions. An unfamiliar smell spreads through the room; remedies from the Caucasus, I think.

Then I stop thinking, because it's midnight.

The baby is resting, asleep on Ivan's shoulder. Ivan pins him against his body like a war medal, pacing from one side of the room to the other.

Ah! I touch my cheeks. There are no thoughts, but there are tears.

Now, an hour later, Ivan is asking me why. He's still carrying the baby.

I try to find a number. I want to be precise. But there is no number for *lie* among Celeste's old code; 17 is misfortune, 90 is fear, but neither of those will do.

The sky was very close, it was a hollowed out hand. Hours had passed, and night had well and truly fallen. A white point appeared at the far end of the road. I waited for it to turn into two headlights, which it did. It couldn't be a motorbike, or a truck, because of the height of the headlights. It was a car, and it was slowing down, as if the motor were slowly dying. I didn't move off the white line in the middle of the road, where I stood balancing with my feet very close together. When the car stopped beside me, Ivan's arm appeared from the window and formed a friendly lasso around my waist.

'Because it's a lie, it's another man's child. And I should never have done this. I swore I'd always tell you the truth. Didn't I?'

The back of Ivan's head says *yes*, and now I understand that I was right from the beginning: he *is* a beautiful monster, the back of his head can speak and see and it is all knowing.

'Let's replay what happened in the desert that night. It's the last thing I'll ever ask of you. Then you can go, or I'll go. Whatever you say, it will be alright.'

Then he comes over. We sit down on the hard floor of the bedroom, full of stones, it seems. And he places an arm around my waist. He doesn't say a word. But I understand the message of his arm. It says: Just after midday the car started again. He continued driving. He looked for me in the desert hotel. He went back to the highway several times, risking another breakdown. But he did not abandon me, not ever, not like those men who abandon their women in small desert towns.

MARIANA DIMÓPULOS was born in Buenos Aires in 1973. She studied literature at the University of Buenos Aires and philosophy at the University of Heidelberg. She is the author of three novels, including *All My Goodbyes*, as well as a critical study on the work of Walter Benjamin. She is a translator from German and English into Spanish and teaches at the University of Buenos Aires.

ALICE WHITMORE's translations from Spanish to English include Mariana Dimópulos's *All My Goodbyes*. Her translation of *Imminence* won the NSW Premier's Translation Prize.

Transit Books is a nonprofit publisher of international and American literature, based in Oakland, California. Founded in 2015, Transit Books is committed to the discovery and promotion of enduring works that carry readers across borders and communities. Visit us online to learn more about our forthcoming titles, events, and opportunities to support our mission.

TRANSITBOOKS.ORG